I0782117

SOFIA

ABOVE THE CLOUDS

By

TERRY BIGGAR

Dedication

I dedicate this book, to my Family and friends.

About the Book

Meet Sofia. She's young, beautiful, and an Airline Hostess for merely a few years. One day, unexpectedly she falls upon a great opportunity. The chance to travel the world. This new opportunity is exciting, it could possibly open windows to a whole new life. This is the beginning of a whole new world. Where will it take her? Will she find her dreams? Come fly with her.

So, sit back and relax because you're here to enjoy *Sofia's Adventures!*

Terry L Biggar

Contents

Chapter 1

"Sofia," a voice called out my name as I fixed my name badge on top of my bright blue vest.

"Coming, just give me two minutes," I responded just as loudly as the person who had called me.

"Your flight is on time!" The voice said, "and it's on gate 2, so you must- "the person talking to me said but before she completed it, I ran out of the bathroom as I realized the urgency of the situation. Leaving everything behind I started to run. And, to make matters worse I was running in my heels.

There WAS no time. My flight was about to depart, and I had been on the other end of the terminal fixing my hair, my outfit and just about everything. Desperately I tugged at the hat—my skirt, and vest I was wearing. It was my uniform, my most prized possession ever since the day I had become an airhostess, and I was cleaning orange juice from it that a passenger had splashed on it which is why I was running late for my connecting flight.

In my brief career, this was the first time I had done

something so careless which made me late.

In fact, not just late but very late. But I wasn't going to give up. Trying to beat time I started to run as fast as I could, and the announcements for my flight started going off. I started to think of the worst-case scenario. In case I didn't make it in time.

My mind started to churn negative thoughts faster than my feet could hit the ground. "No Sofia, you can't think of bad things," I tried giving myself confidence. This is your first mistake, anyone can ignore first time offenders right, I said to myself again, but my brain clearly disagreed as it showed no signs of agreeing with me,

As I ran past the gates, and I saw a lot of people heading to their own gates I finally saw the opening that said "2". There were a group of people waiting to board the plane, a man, attractive, his hair black and slightly longish, with a pair of thick edged glasses framing narrowed eyes. There was a girl alongside him, carrying a ton of bags.

I ran past them, in a hurry, and entered the gate.

Good morning, Sofia, the security guard said to me as I passed him with a gentle yet embarrassed smile.

Hurry ... hurry sweetheart, they`re waiting for you.

"Sorry," I muttered and pouted my lips.

He quickly scanned my bag and waved me on.

I had carefully boarded the plane just on time. I was on board, and yet I felt my heart still beating fast. The roar of the engines starting up seemed to rise in pitch and volume.

I took my position and gave the safety instructions to the passengers. The seat belt lights came on.

And, in a few minutes the plane took off. I took a long sigh of relief as I looked out the small window. This was one of the pleasant features of being an airhostess.

I remember the day I fell in love with flying.

I so vividly remember; it was my summer vacation, I had boarded a flight with my parents, I was tired, and annoyed with carrying the heavy handbag but once I was seated in the plane, I remember that everything had changed. The weather, which was sunny and mild, was perfect for flying. I was merely twelve or thirteen, and when the plane took off, I could see the gardens and the blooming flowers around the airport, as if it was part of an intricate bouquet. It was beautiful.

There was a very sweet airhostess who helped me throughout the flight. Never had an airhostess tried to comfort me on a flight; usually they looked away. But not this airhostess she was different. She was beautiful and sweet, I liked her and her simple, yet necessary affirmation had helped me calm down.

That was the day I decided this is what I wanted to do when I was of age to do so.

At the age of twenty-one I was determined to be one of the top Hostesses. This was the life I had chosen for me. And I was going to do my best to make that happen no matter how.

From the beginning, this is what flying meant to me. It`s where I belong.

I quickly gained composure and managed to get all the passengers settled in for their flight. The captain's voice came on giving the weather details and time of arrival.

Up above a thirty-thousand-foot perspective when from the corner of my just a few feet away I noticed a man. There was a nice-looking man…roughly my age, or a little older, that I was working with today.

A strong jaw, dark eyes. He is what you would call 'too good-looking' in a British film star kind of way. Ashton was on his name badge.

I love that name I thought to myself.

We exchanged greetings, and carried on with our duty`s.

A routine flight as usual. We did end up with some ***turbulence…nothing heavy…but that was short lived.***

Coffee was served, with an assortment of small snacks.

Soon after, it was time to clear everything up again.

Ashton had fewer passengers in his area….so he came to offer help with mine. He appeared at my side, with the beverage cart. "Let me help you" he said, and the warm, richly masculine sound of his voice comforted me.

I smiled and nodded. Thank You

What a nice man.

We introduced ourselves, and some pleasantries.

It was so nice to meet a young personable, and considerate man, who was around my age, maybe a year or two older.

We completed our few commuter flights back and forth, and then said our goodbyes.

Nice meeting you Ashton…. Yes, same here Sofia.

Have a great night.

I headed out and hailed a taxi home.

I decided to also make a stop for some Chinese for dinner. The taxi driver was accommodating.

"That's it, for me," Cary says, picking up one of the many blankets that were on the floor. "These people have no manners," she said a little annoyed. 'I am tired, and I really need to go home now." Cary complained again as she dropped the blanket on the aisle.

It was a rough group today. Everyone seemed irritable and demanding. They made a mess of the plane.

By the end of our shift, we were exhausted.

I pick up the fallen blanket and tried to hand it back to her. "Just a few more rows," I say. "The guy who was working with me in the last flight, helped me tidy up the whole plane," I said remembering close-ups of his dark eyes, & handsome face.

"Yes, yes I know Ashton helped you…I have heard the story twenty times since yesterday," Cary winked and smiled, and I laughed. 'I am just saying, it doesn't take that long." I rearrange my pout to a smile

"I know but Sofia, I am not twenty like you," she mopes, "I am getting old lol." "Okay, okay I won't try to convince you, the clean-up crew is almost here," I said, and Cary smiled in victory. She was in no mood of tidying up the plane with me. She already had on her coat and was making her way towards

The door when she tossed the blankets to the floor.

"When Holden comes, tell him the floor is where he'll find the blankets," she says. 'Or if you're lucky maybe Ashton will come, and you two can use the blankets?" she glances back over her shoulder at me and winks. "

I stared at Cary for a few moments, then laughed, "Keep your imaginations to yourself! and as for Holden, he isn't working today, his dad had surgery. So, he won't be back until next week." I said, recalling the conversation I had with Holden when I saw him on last flight. Holden was the head of aircraft cabin cleaning, who was usually assigned our flights.

They worked at night, when we were done for the day. They did a deeper cleaning., which is why it was normal for Cary to assume he would be on his way.

"Then ask who`s ever shift it is to clean up when he comes in... I've worked with you enough to know that you probably know the name of every person who works on the plane."

That makes me laugh. "Riley. That's the guy you're thinking of," I reminded her. Cary shrugs. "Yeah. Riley."

"You know it wouldn't be so bad if you remembered the name of the people you work with too." I joked, and Cary rolled her eyes and opened the aircraft's door. O K... I`m off.

See you tomorrow maybe. I think we`re on together, but if not… have a great day.

"Wait. You're coming next Saturday, right?" Maina wanted me to bring my 'other friends'?" Maina had suggested we do a friend-giving while I was in the city on Thanksgiving break.

My friends Fredric and Ricardo were going to host and BBQ Which means we'll probably end up ordering Chinese food. LOL. They had many talents… but BBQ was one of them LOL.

There`ll be Angel.,. Kayley. And Me and Ricardo   and Fredric of course lol and you. Also, I think Peter is coming if he isn`t working.

You`ve worked with him, right?

Yes, many times. he`s great.

Ok I`ll see what I can do to make it.

That would be nice Cary." I said as I folded the last blanket.

I`ll let you know she replies.

Ok… I`m done. I`ll see you soon. Good night.

Cary leaves.

The door that was just shut closed by Cary a few minutes ago flies open and a woman emerges. She was wearing a bright print dress, and she had ginger locks.

"Miss., Can I help you?" I asked as she entered.

"Yes, I am looking for Sofia,"

"I am Sofia," I said, keeping my eyes firmly on her.

"Oh," O k "You are wanted in the head office," she

I was suddenly very tired, exhausted from cleaning and tidying everything up after a very trying day.

Oh. is there something wrong? I questioned

No... I don`t think so. "I've been asked to call you right now," I stared at her, startled by the urgency of this call up.

My heart started to pound.

"Oh okay," I said as I straightened myself up.

She smiled at me then "Great,"

As I walked outside the plane and inside the airport, moving a quick pace with the woman who was accompanying me, my eyes aimed at my own feet, shoulders tense, walking steadfastly unaware of why I was called for.

By the time I had walked twenty or so steps, my back started to ache. I felt an immediate, intense need to stop walking and just ask her what was going on.

"You know why they want me?" I asked, and I saw the back of her head nod sideways.

"No. But it seems important.

My stomach twisted, and I moved quickly as I followed closely behind her. As I came close to the conference room office, Kyle, the receptionist stood up from his seat and greeted me pleasantly by name.

"Good afternoon, Miss Sofia." He shot me a pleasant grin.

"Hi Kyle," I said as I tried my best to sound confident. The woman who I was following gave him a nod and I saw the conference room door in front of my eyes.

Please go inside." the woman pointed towards the large wooden door and stopped in her heels.

"Good luck Miss Sofia," Kyle said, I sighed and mouthed a thank you.

Be calm, be sensible, be cool, I repeated to myself.

With a slightly trembling hand, I reached for the door handle and opened it. `

I was greeted by three people. All of them in their fifties- all three of them oozing tremendous power and steely control.

One of the men sat at the head of the table, which was set perpendicular to the length of the table, the other two sat on his right. Facing him sideways.

"Hi, Ms. Di Carlo." one of the men inside the room said.

His face looked familiar.

He was in his early fifties, dressed impeccably, with both his shirt and tie in a soft gray that perfectly complimented his black blazer.

"I am great, how are you? I asked as I took a deep breath, feeling like I was in for a lecture.

"We're okay as well," the first man, who responded, radiating an impression of powerful demand.

Please have a seat Ms. Di Carlo." the woman in the room said, as she headed towards the seat in front of the table.

My stomach quivered, "Yes- "

"I mean thank you," I said as I sat in front of the woman and the man, and to the right of the head, who was sitting with his arms folded. It was an awkward position, but I was not one to complain so I just smiled and looked in their eyes. I tried not to fidget.

My name is Frank Davis, this is Howard Scott, and that is Barbara Newman,"

Frank, the first man pointed towards the other two people, and I smiled nervously.

"We have called you hear because we wanted to talk to you about a recent development.

Oh no. They want to talk about the near flight miss I had.

Startled, I blinked. "Okay," I gulped, "what about it?"

"Well, firstly we wanted to congratulate you for being one of the best performing airhostesses of our airline,"

We take great pride in our airline and recognize hard

working employees.

"And secondly we wanted to offer you an opportunity,"

"What kind of opportunity," My fingers curled around the ends of my chair's armrests and the air left my lungs in a rush, followed immediately by every bit of common sense I possessed.

"Well, "His gaze held mine, we`d love to offer you "the opportunity to be an airhostess at Exotic Airlines," I`m sure you must have heard of it?

Yes, I have   I said fighting the lump that was forming in my throat.

"We want you to come work at Exotic Airlines, we think your talents and professionalism, would be perfect for our private line.

Sofia froze.

I wanted his take on it all. But when he finished, I was quiet.

Dead quiet.

Frank looked at me, waiting, expectant. I could see the muscle flex in his jaw as he looked at me. I searched for words that wouldn't come.

"Sofia?" he took my name and between astonished joy and bewilderment. I lifted my head to look at him and found him bright-eyed and smiling. "Well, what do you say?"

"I am sorry Mr. Davis, I am just at a loss for words,"

"To be honest, I am overwhelmed,"

He laughed and a familiar warm, richly masculine sound resounded in my ears.

In a good way, I hope?

Do you have any questions? or reservations?

No… Not at all.

'So, does that mean you don't want to come to Exotic Airlines?"

"No, no, I'd be honored to."

Great We`ll go over the details,

"Well," Barbara said in her calm, voice. "This Private Airline is kept extremely exclusive, available to only the most elite. which means you'll be serving some of the wealthiest figures in the world as well as top private groups, and business executives.

Here`s just a brief rundown.

"As for the benefits, you'll get your own room in some of the best resorts wherever you are.

You'll get a clothing allowance and have access to transportation around the area. Of course, you`ll receive a nice pay raise as well.

This is a dream opportunity.

Sofia sits in awe.

"Is there anything you'd like to be added?" Mr. Davis asked. "Just say the word, & we'll do our best.," I shook my head: no

"This is great," I cover my mouth to hide my excitement, "everything…everything sounds great," I answered, with a satisfied smile.

I`ve only been here roughly three years. I`m amazed that you see potential in me. I have tried to do my best with every flight. I love people... I love making them feel important, no matter where they came from.

Yes... and it has been noticed. We appreciate employees like yourself.

"So… Sofia Di Carlo if everything is set, let's get you an employment contract?" Frank said confidently, and I nodded my head.

"Perfect," he pursed his lips, "Kyle will help you with it,"

"Thank you Mr. Davis I am looking forward to it," I said as I grinned ear to ear.

"One last thing, Miss Di Carlo," Frank asked me, with a warm smile plastered on his face, as I looked at him expectantly,

"Welcome aboard Exotic Airlines,"

The moment he said that a tight-lipped blonde in a sleek business suit opened the door and stepped inside the office

As she led me from the conference room, my head was spinning with all the possibilities and opportunities.

I will have a chance of travelling with exotic airlines.

Thank You very much, Mr. Davis. I will give 100 %.

You won`t regret giving me the opportunity.

As they said their goodbyes. Barbara mentioned to Sophia that she will have roughly a week to get prepared for the first trip. Her new uniform will be delivered in a couple of days. Sophia was excited. She headed home and right away started calling her friends.

Still in disbelief. She gave each of them a rundown of her great news. She explained that she would be very busy and that they will all get together after her first trip. There was so much to do. She will call them again when she had more details.

The following day, a messenger delivered a large business envelope. Inside was her contract, along with other details and information. The one paper had a description of how the trips would work. Number one, the clients will receive the highest quality of food, drinks and service

White glove.

Number two, the staff does not speak to the clients unless they are spoken to. Three Upon arriving at their destination, the clients will be greeted with their limos to take them to their private destination. Then once, they've left the premises. A limo will then arrive for the rest of the crew, where you'll be taken to your beautiful resort.

The plane remains for the duration, ready for any side trips if need be. While Sofia read with surprise, there was more info and rules. Okay, I'd better practice my smooth, cool royalty service moves and get ready for the change. She finished reading everything and signed the bottom as directed. She checked the envelope and found that one last note in big, bold letters that read Get ready for ROME!

Oh, my God. Awesome, she thought. Then it gave weather details and a variety of things that she could do places to go and see. Oh, I'm so excited, Sophia thought.

Oh, my God. As she puts down the papers, I must get prepared now. The next few days she spent checking her wardrobe, facetiming her friends and planning. Yvonne was called and agreed very happily to bring in her mail and water, her flowers and plants. Yvonne is her neighbor.

Soon…in a flash, came the night before her first Exotic trip.

OK... I took care of everything I needed to, and I`m ready to go!

Sophia decides to go to bed early and get a real good night's sleep.

I smoothed my hands over my hair and try to catch a glimpse of my reflection in the glass door as I step inside the airport. Our uniforms are a female version of a Tuxedo.

It does kind of suit me I must say.

After passing through security, the doors begin to open.

My heart flutters down my chest. My first Exotic Airlines flight, my first destination -ROME ITALY

. Here we come!

I was greeted by the captain and copilot.

Two nice looking men I must say.

Kaylee came over and gave me a hug.

I was surprised to see her! She informed me that she does

part time with Exotic as well as the other.

Sofia felt a little more relaxed.

We immediately started with the Safety procedures.

The captain announced ... prepare for Takeoff.

The roar of engines grew louder.

Once we reached our altitude, we began with drinks.

The Alcohol was of all high-priced brands. Very exclusive and some rare bottles of wine. Mostly European.

The menu was pure indulgence! unlike anything I had experienced before. A luxury that I could have only hoped in my dreams. The guests were very distinguished looking. They were served the most expensive drinks and exquisite plates of fruit and cheese that had my mouth watering. Even the insides of the plane smelled heavenly!

An hour later we brought out the main meals.

The choices were ***

1. Lobster bisque, with Lobster tails and linguini

2. Steak with baby roasted potatoes, and asparagus tips

3. Chicken parmesan, with fettuccini.

Each meal also came with their choice of salads, and fresh artisan breads.

It was my first flight, and everything felt surreal. Even my interaction with the other attendants. I was with Kaylee. She was beautiful & so professional that I could not help but admire her. I could see why she was hired and apart from her apparent beauty & professionalism, she was well-spoken. I had worked with her many times. She was teaching me what to do and what not to do. I was a great air hostess, but the observations I made about her behavior made me more confident. And, since this was a new experience, I wanted to work extra hard.

"Sophia, do you want to take a break?" Kaylee asked me.

"No, thank you," I answer politely as I pour a drink of white wine for a guest.

She smiles.

"You're clearly very motivated and excited,"

My face broke into an embarrassing smile.

"Is that obvious?" I asked, hiding my cheeky grin.

"No, but I am great at reading faces," she said and winked at me.

"I haven't been this excited about my life since that Coldplay concert I attended last year."

"Well, maybe we can top that with a Coldplay concert in flight?"

"LOL, I don't think that's possible," I said lightly.

"Everything is possible at exotic airlines," she says with a wink, "trust me, you're in for more surprises,"

And as she said that I could not help but wonder if she was serious or joking with a newbie. As time went and the flight continued, I experienced things that were giving birth to butterflies in my stomach. The flight was long, it was tiring but the passengers, they were like royalty. & that's how we were supposed to treat them.

Soon, a lot of the passengers were sleeping.

This gave us the chance to relax for a while.

The captain came on again. This time announcing our descent into Rome.

We quickly prepared for landing.

The passengers slowly awoke and started to look out the windows. The lights were amazing.

ROME

The moment I set foot in Rome; I feel adventurous. A car was here to pick us up and take us to the hotel that was more than 40 minutes away. Hotel de Rossie; it was one of Rome's most exclusive hotels with rooms always being booked and one room going for more than three thousand dollars a night.

Apparently, that's where Kaylee and I were staying. We arrive at the enormous – and frankly intimidating and lavish – glass, steel, and white sandstone hotel lobby.

It was dark out and we were tired.

We checked in and decided to make it an early night.

The room I was given, was spacious, bright, and elegant. It was a mix of classic and contemporary styles.

I showered and climbed into bed and soon fell asleep with the TV.

The next morning, I awoke refreshed and ordered up coffee. I started to explore my room with its Italian style décor.

But as beautiful as the room was, I wasn't planning on staying inside for too long. I called Kaylee's room but got no answer. So, I wandered out into the hotel. I rang Kaylee's phone again, to ask her if she wanted to come and go across the city and explore but she still wasn't in her room. She was down in the gym. That's what she asked me to do as well. I said maybe tomorrow.

So, I decided to go city gazing on my own. Filled with excitement, I asked for a car.

The first thing I did in Italy was go shopping. I found a few different shops and purchased a bikini, hat, and matching sarong.

Afterward, I took a drive along a winding road, with views of the crystal blue waters. The scenery was breathtaking! I spotted a small café, where I decided to stop, and have a bite to eat. I ordered a glass of wine, and a croissant. There were grape vineyards for miles. I sat in amazement for quite some time, trying to believe I was really in Rome.

Soon I decided to head back to the Resort.

As I made my way out of the cute little café, I could sense there was someone following me. I pushed a fistful of hair out of my eyes to look behind me, when I saw a light blue color shirt behind me. It was a police officer. I couldn't see his face, but my entire body tingled with anxiety. Just pretend you're from here and he won't do anything. You're not doing anything wrong.

As I approached my car. I could hear his footsteps behind me getting closer. I turned around and asked if I did anything wrong.

No dear. I was watching you inside and found you so beautiful! Your long blonde hair was shining in the sunlight.

I want to get to know you better. Can I buy you dinner?

Sofia stopped. No thank you. I`m spoken for. (She lied)

Oh, please madam! I want to show you a good time, as they say.

No thank you sir…please leave me alone!

I got in the car and drove back to the resort without stopping.

Up in my room I sort through my purchases. I bought enough wine, for myself and my friends. I packed them neatly in my suitcase, separating them and wrapping them in the middle with my clothes so they won't break. I tried calling Kaylee again, and this time she answered.

Oh, great you`re back. Come to my room.

A few minutes later there was a knock on her door. Kaylee entered.

Hey! I thought maybe we could call a taxi and have him take us to the finest Italian restaurant in the area. Are you getting hungry?

I`m famished Kaylee replied. I`m in the mood for gnocchi! That sounds good Sofia replies. I might like some Fettuccine Alfredo! Mmm.

Off they went. There was a cozy little Pasta and wine café just about 3 miles away. Just the perfect place for our first real Italian experience.

 The aroma was insane.

They ordered and sipped some wine.

Chapter 6

'Sophia, the city is literally bursting! It has everything from museums, historical sites, restaurants, tours, classes, and more.

We are going to be very busy. We should make a list of important things to do.

"Yeah, I'd like to do all of that, but I am not sure where to start,"

Her lips arch with a trace of a smile, "its set now, we're going together tomorrow. We'll start with the Eternal City's most-famous places so we can cross them off our bucket list. Then we'll take a few classes maybe find a fabulous Gelato Bar, and flirt with some pretty Italian guys!" she smiles, her eyes twinkling with the spark of adventure.

"Perfect," I say as I finish dinner.

Then as both Kaylee and I finish the wonderful dinner we hailed a taxi back to the hotel.

Wow what a meal! I think that did me in for the night.

We`ll have an early start, after a light breakfast.

O K, Sofia yawned. Jet lag is starting to hit me. I think I`ll just relax the rest of the evening and catch up on some sleep.

"Me too, Kaylee agrees.

She hugs me.

"I'm glad we're here together, let's meet tomorrow at 8am and we'll start our adventures together." She wanders back down the corridor, and straight to her room.

Chapter 7

The City of Rome

The next morning, I woke up with the biggest smile on my face. The mornings in Rome were Different. They were chilly but, during the day, when the sun was out, it was perfect!

So, as I freshened up, I got dressed in a jean jacket. T shirt. And Jeans. I paired them with the boots and big shades that complimented my face and a light scarf- for color. Dressed in my touristy look we started off to discover Rome.

"We must find a Gelato Bar! she stated excitedly, and I nodded. Sure! I am up for it," I said and that's where we went. Kaylee had a soul of an adventurer. We sat enjoying our authentic Gelato. We sat in front of the window that overlooked a magnificent Fountain. There were tourists everywhere.

Come on Kaylee…lets go throw a coin in the fountain and make a wish! Ok…lets. `

We both took out our cell phones, which we had loaded up with data of course, and began taking selfies.

OMG what cool pictures we got. At one point, Kaylee almost fell into the water! LOL

We were told to visit some museums as well. I`m not one for museums, but we did go to one we spotted on the way.

WOW….it was breathtaking! The works of art were beyond beautiful. It was just like everyone said.

Hamm maybe I do like them after all!

The masterpieces were beyond words. How do people have such unbelievable talents such as these painting! They were all breathtaking! We were there for hours it seemed.

We decided to head back, and lounge around the pool Kaylee suggested checking in on some classes for Pizza making. We inquired at the concierge in our hotel.

There was one not to far away, and we signed up for the next morning.

Great!   10.00 am.

Ok... lets have a light dinner and relax for the evening. Tomorrow will be busy.

Our meals were simply wonderful…. we were both stuffed to

the brim.

All right, it`s time to retire.

Soo much excitement. Let's meet up around 8.00 for breakfast.

They said their good nights and entered their rooms.

Morning came, and the girls met at the same restaurant in the hotel.

Are you ready for Pizza making? Sofia`s eyes light up.

Oh Yaa…. Kaylee responds.

They ate and then wondered around the hotel, until it was time to leave.

They called for a taxi and were soon at Papa Vince's.

He greeted them warmly with hugs and kisses and brought them to a back kitchen.

Wow! Kaylee beamed with delight. This is fully equipped.

I see this says Sofia. Very professional.

O K Ladies… I`ma gonna teach you some of my best dough recipes for Pizza. You will love them.

They watched with intense eyes and took notes.

Afterwards they were able to try themselves.

They couldn`t believe they did it.

O M G! we made perfect pizza dough.

 Now for the toppings.

Papa Vince handed them each a sheet of the most amazing combinations they ever saw.

They each picked one… and finished their Pizza.

He then sat them at a table to enjoy their creations.

This is amazing the girls shouted!

Ima glad you approve Papa Vince replied.

Thank You so much for the lesson! Sofia gleamed.

Oh, you a welcome my beauty.

We`ll remember this experience for ever.

They hugged and kissed, and the girls took what's left of their

Pizza back to their hotel.

They changed and went to sit out at the pool.

Ok.... we should inquire about cheese making.

I`d love that!

They called down to the front desk and found what they wanted. They planned for the next day 11.00am.

This was at an authentic cheese house.

Mozzarella, and Ricotta.

After a long swim, and a couple glasses of wine...They took a walk around the hotel. It was a masterpiece in itself! The atmosphere was intoxicating! Then they decided to relax for the evening.

The next morning, they repeated there day, only with cheese.

They made it the old school way., and it was cool. They were able to make quite a lot...and paid for more to take back for their friends. Sofia never forgets her best friends.

Wow... fresh Italian cheese. What a treat!

They decided to fit in some shopping., so they hailed a taxi and had him take them to a nice mall.

They both left with multiple bags lol. We are shopaholics lol.

How about we stop for some Gelato Kaylee asks.

Yes, sounds good to me.

The taxi whisked them off and brought them to a quaint little Gelato café.

They ordered an expresso each and chose their flavor for the Gelato.

Pure heaven … Kaylee sighed. Wow! Maybe it`s a good thing, we don`t have it this good in New York lol.

Ok … I`m done for the day. I think I`ll hit the gym, then just relax tonight, with a book I brought. I think we should tour a few wineries this week.

I agree Sofia replied. Let's check into that tomorrow.

Great. Let's head back.

Tomorrow another adventure awaits!

As the next day started, we began with a light breakfast by the pool.

I was dressed in a new silk suit. It was a Last-minute purchase.

The light pink color, almost like a rose wine. It hugged my curves perfectly.

We signed up for a fabulous wine tour.

There was a large group leaving at 1.00 PM

We just wondered around our resort and walked outside into the most beautiful gardens I had ever seen.

We took fabulous pictures and a few selfies of course.

I think our phones are getting full lol.

Soon it was time to go. We got on the shuttle and headed out to the wineries.

As we arrived, we were greeted with a smile by this distinguished-looking man who made us feel comfortable and welcome

Everyone seems so warm here…Like family!

I just could not stop grinning. Italy had given me something that I craved for so long. Memories…fun and so much to learn from. It felt like home.

I could say easily that in all my life, I had never seen anything quite like Rome.

The tour was so interesting. We were given samples of some of their best vintages. We also purchased some to take home.

That was awesome. What a treat.

This was our final day. We were able to do most of what we had hoped to do.

Kaylee and I decided to have dinner at the same place where we went the first night. Just to commemorate this wonderful trip.

"This last dinner feels so sad." Kaylee sighs, and I nod my head in agreement. "True,"

"I mean, really, even though we're technically here for work, what a trip it has been," she swirls her fork and wraps the spaghetti on it as she sucks it in one go, And... "I'm sad to leave behind, gelato, and the pretty cafes," says Kaylee.

"Me too; maybe one day we can return & enjoy more than just creepy policemen hitting on us."

"Just you Hun, no policeman hit on me, & trust me, I have tried," Kaylee said, and I burst into laughter. I'm glad she was busy eating her food because my face is on fire.

The next day comes, and I get ready for my flight. It was early in the morning, I call Kaylee to the lobby, and we have breakfast in the hotel café.

Baked eggs and sausage, with the best tiramisu I had ever tried then I was finally reminded by Kaylee that it was time to go.

After breakfast, we ride back to the airport.

"Just like I had never left," I grunt, and Kaylee looks at me, "missing the tiramisu?" She asks, and I nod my head. "More than anything,"

'Well, I hope you're able to forget that tiramisu with a good gizzada or coconut drops, or maybe a sweet potato pudding, you know they're heavenly," she said, and I just looked at her with a question mark on my face.

"Wait, I don't know any of the foods you just mentioned,"

Kaylee scrunched up her lips and thought for a second. "You haven't been told?" she says, and I shake my head. "Not really?" I said, unsure of what she was talking about. 'Babe, you are going to JAMAICA! she said, and I squealed a little.

Yaa, I got an email just before leaving my room. I thought you would have seen it too.

"What?" I said in amazement, and she nodded her head. "Yep, and I have heard the cabin crew they picked for the flight is extra attractive, so I know why you're going," she added that with a smirk that seemed *almost* like a wink.

I smiled. "God, you're too much."

She patted my back as she laughed. "Oh, this is nothing,"

Once on board the plane, we look out the windows as we see the last view of such a beautiful country. Not only was it stunning, but it was also Mysterious.

Like God had made this city with a lot of thought, detail, and attention. But, we had to go.

Thankfully, the return flight was smooth and uneventful. Everyone on the flight was rather tired. Which meant I didn't really need to cater to any peculiar demands. Except a few requests from two of the VIP guests. They just couldn't decide what they wanted.

"My companion prefers coffee, black." One of the two guests kept repeating, when the friend who he was ordering for would interfere. "Yes, I prefer coffee, but I'll have brandy."

This happened for the whole flight, I would pour coffee, I'd be asked to bring brandy. I'd bring brandy and they'd ask me to bring coffee. It went back and forth for a while until Kaylee came to my rescue and I was free. Other than that, all the passengers were super sweet. The flight landed, and we went to work cleaning. Once finished, we head out and go through customs. No problems thank God! We picked up our bags and I took my phone out of my pocket and opened UBER. I stared at the blank map on my Uber app.

"You want a ride home?" Kaylee asked and I shook my head. "No Thank You. I have my own personal chauffer you see," I waved the mobile phone with the uber app in her face, and she chuckled. 'Okay,"

"BYE, KAYLEE," I said loudly as I walked out of the airport, "I really hope to see you soon sometime! "I waved my hand as I got into the car.

"You will, hopefully we're scheduled on the same flight to Jamaica," I hear her voice through the door of my car. "Hopefully, if not I don't know what I'll do," I mumble under my breath. I love working with her.

Back home, everything was exactly as I had left it: utterly

clean and fresh. I took off my heels, changed into one of my sweat suits.

I made a coffee and sat out on the balcony. It was beautiful out and I sat quietly reminiscing about Italy!

Suddenly the ring of my phone startled me.

"Ciao Perdure Sofia," she says seductively, and I burst into laughter.

"Why are you laughing?" Maina says, clearly offended that her greeting made me laugh.

"Because you dummy Perdrera means, MISS, like I miss you, not miss like the prefix," I say as I try to believe that she just said that.

"Ooops, I guess that's what I get for learning Italian from google translate and not Pedrera Ginevra," I smile amusingly

 How was Italy?" She asked, and I bit my lip.

"Uneventful," I lie, and she catches up on it.

"Stop lying; I know you're biting your lip…you can't make me believe that someone as YOU gorgeous went to Bel Pavese and didn't do anything,"

My jaw tightens at that accusation, an accurate allegation. "I am telling you the truth," I said, and I could picture her shaking her head in disagreement through the phone.

"I am calling the others, and we're all meeting up, OKAY?"

"Oh yes! but I am going to Jamaica next, so we have to schedule a meet up before that," I said.

"Oh Jamaica! Awesome!

"Yes, Jamaica,

"Tomorrow, at Alexanders with the boys," I heard her squeal & before I could agree, she hung up.

Tomorrow at Alexanders it is then.

I was Happy I opened my laptop's browser and Googled "MUST SEE DESTINATIONS IN JAMAICA."

My next stop, and what I didn't knew now my most important stop where I'd meet someone important. *Or re meet.*

Chapter 8

Dinner with the friends

I let my blonde hair down and flowing around my shoulders. I wore neat, pointed pumps, black casual pants, and a loose fitted sweater.

I walked out of my apartment. Alexanders was close to where I lived so I decided to walk to the restaurant.

As I entered, I searched through dimly lit tables for my friends, my gaze skipped over tables occupied by couples, some businessmen, a few women for their lady's night. As my eyes scanned the tables one after another that's when I spotted Maina's. She was already there, and with her were Fredrick Grant, and Ricardo Baro, my favorite couple in the whole wide world.

They already had their wine glasses in their hands, and they were already talking about something. Probably about how I was always late. As I walked closer to the table with the biggest smile on my face. I heard someone's high pitched voice micromanaging the waiter on how the wine was not the perfect amount of cold.

I turned around to see who it was. It was Peter, another one of my friends. He had been with me as a cabin manager when I started out but now, he was in modelling because of well, his immaculate fashion sense and good looks.

'Look who finally decided to show up," he said as he turned around and spotted me.

"Miss Exotic, SOFIA!" he announced as if I was the winner of an academy award. Maina, Ricardo and Fredrick all turned around at the sound of his announcement and started clapping their hands.

"Guys I'm literally just 10 minutes late, I'm sorry… I said in my defense, but my friends were just glad to see me.

"Well, it's because you always liked to make an entrance," Maina added, "And she does it well." Ricardo added as he looked at me up and down, judging my look.

"If I wasn't gay or if Fredrick wasn't here, I would totally hit on you," he said, and I laughed.

"But I am here Ricardo…and you are GAY!" Fredrick cleared his throat and the whole table burst into laughter.

You`re an ASS!

But…You`re right…she looks amazing in that outfit.

Maybe I`ll hit on her…. LOL…JUST KIDDING!

God, it was going to be a great night.

The entire evening was fun filled with a lot of good food, stories and wine. I got a bit of slack for forgetting my friends as I got my new job, but it wasn't anything that I could not have handled.

"So, how true is it that pilots hit on airhostesses," peter asked, and I giggled.

"Well, in my case it's not true at all," I said as I took a sip of my wine, "everyone I have met has been super sweet and not at all flirty,"

"I can't believe a word of it, a pretty girl like you and no pilot has hit on you. Just not true."

'Trust me, I am telling the truth,"

"So, no scandal? How boring," Fredrick said as he made a face. That's when I heard a denial from the end of the table,

"Well not a pilot…... but there IS this guy Ashton that I heard her gush over,"

Before I could say anything in my defense, Ricardo butted in.

"Ashton…sounds SAUCY,"

Oh…I know him. Peter stated. and I crossed my arms over my chest as I smiled. Or tried to.

"He's no one… Maina just likes the drama," I said but Maina shook her head.

"No one?... that's not what I think.

"Maina I think the gin is making you a little fuzzy.

"SO, he is no one?" Peter asked,

"Well, he is a person, technically not a no one. "

"So, is this person cute?" the questions piled, and I took a big gulp.

"What I meant to say— yes he's a person, but not a person that I have anything to do with,"

"Yet!" Fredrick said as he winked. And I turned red.

Listen guy`s... You`ll be the first to know, when and if there`s anything to tell. OK?

Now… I think I should head home. I have a lot to do this week before leaving again.

Yaa that sounds good to me too Ricardo adds. We were busy today. And on top of that, we had Yoga first thing this morning. The instructor killed us Uggggh.

O k… Good night, guy`s…. we can keep in touch by phone. I won`t have time to get together.

Awe sweety we`ll miss you again!

Let`s do a face time soon. For sure Hun. Sofia whined.

Let us give you a ride!   No, that`s ok I`ll walk. I want to keep in shape lol. Thanks anyway guy`s. Love You!!!!!

Chapter 9

The next morning, I woke up with the streaming sunlight shinning in my bedroom, the beautiful scene was broken when a rumbling sound came from my stomach.

"Ugh," I moan as I remember the night, I had just had with my friends… What a great night it was, so many things to talk about and so much to eat I thought as I stretched around in my bed. I was just thinking when my stomach rumbled again. *Boy was I hungry*, which was surprising because I had enough food last night for the entire week. Yet my stomach wanted more1

I thought back to the fantastic Chicken Parmigiana I had yesterday in memory of Italy. But as I thought back to it, it is something I probably shouldn't have had, because it made me reminisce about Italy.

For a while, I lie there on my bed with the sunlight creeping inside my window.

But then, as I rolled around in bed, I looked at the clock staring at my face.

If I didn't get up now, I'd be getting to lazy for my chores and I want to check my wardrobe for Jamaica.

I got up from the bed, looked at my phone that was charging on the bedside table beside me and picked it up to write down my list of things to do I placed my hands on the keypad and started typing;

I. Drop off uniform at the dry cleaners
II. Organize my suitcase according to weather in Jamaica
III. Check on my bathing suits
IV. Check with Yvonne to come water my plants and pick up my mail
V. Google Jamaica for things to see and do.
VI. Try and get into my hairdressers!

After writing down my list of things to do I made my way to the bathroom to take a shower and get dressed.

LET'S START THIS DAY

I put on a casual but cute buttery yellow dress and paired them with some hammered metal earrings that twinkled in the sunlight and with a hungry stomach I made my way out of the apartment when I noticed someone new settling in the building. There were boxes everywhere on my floor.

"Oh, looks like I am getting a new neighbor," I said to myself excitedly and before I could investigate further my doubt was confirmed when I saw a woman.

"Welcome to the building," I greeted her as her back was towards me.

"Thank you," she turned around pushed a fistful of dark hair out of her eyes and the most stunning pair of coffee-brown eyes stared at me. She was wearing a pair of nice faded grey pants and a casual, pink top. Her hair was in a ponytail, with a few strands falling over her forehead. She was fit but she looked a little older maybe in her early forties.

"Do you need any help?" I asked her as I bend down to pick one of the boxes.

"Oh, thank you," but that`s ok. She lightly tapped my hand away. "I wouldn't want to ruin that beautiful dress plus I am very used to this," I have help, she said as she pointed towards the men that were helping her move in.

"I mean you're my neighbor, anything for you," I said nicely.

"You're too sweet," she said. "Is everyone in this building

as sweet as you…?"

She asked, and I nodded. "I hope so, but if you're looking for someone, I am Sophia," She threw her head back and laughed. "Ok Sophia, I'll definitely keep that in mind, I am Lenora,"

"Lenora, that's a beautiful name.

"Where are you running off to so early in the morning?" she asked me, and I filled her in.

"Just running a few errands. I leave in a few days for Jamaica

"Oh, wonderful!

"Yes, I`m an Airline Hostess… so always on the go.

"Wow that sounds exciting," her eyes were twinkling with excitement.

"It is, I'll tell you about it" later. I smiled,

"I can't wait to hear! When I was young, I wanted to be an airhostess too, but my passions collided and here I am," she chuckled.

"Well, maybe one of these days I can give you a rundown of what it's like to be one," I winked, and she smiled the biggest smile.

"Sounds perfect,"

"Well Lenora, I am glad you're moving in," I said as I looked at her hand. Her knuckles were turning white as she clung onto the box tightly. "I am so sorry; I'm holding you up here.

She laughed and placed the box on the floor. "No worries, dear, I am used to this you please leave I don't want you to be late for your errands,"

"I'll catch up with you when I return from my trip. I'll have you over for a coffee," I said and smiled.

I made my way to a cozy café for my favorite breakfast. A cheese croissant and coffee.

Then set out to conquer some   of my list. Over the next couple of days, I managed to cross everything off.

The few days went by fast, and suddenly it was the morning of my trip.

I woke up extra early… just to re check my suitcase.

I called for a taxi and headed off to the airport. I was cleared with security and was heading for our briefing area when I heard a familiar voice call out my name!

"Ashton? "I said in surprise. Every sensation in my body heightened as he walked closer to me.

"I'm glad you remember my name," he said and released a husky laugh.

"Of course, I do," I said, and he smiled.

"How are you here?" I enquired and his smile turned into a grin.

"Well, if you haven't noticed by the uniform, I'm with you on the Exotic Airlines,"

"Oh, that's a pleasant surprise,"

"Are you sure? Because you look more shocked than pleasantly surprised," he said as he tilted his head and a mischievous grin appeared on his lips again.

"Yes Ashton, I am pleasantly surprised." I said and he arched an eyebrow at me. "In fact, I am happy, I'm glad I have a familiar face around me,"

"I am glad that familiar face is you,"

My stomach twisted in a knot but before I could answer, Ashton started to walk.

"Now let's go inside. We don't want to be late, "and started to walk inside the main entrance. With excitement in my heart and sparkle in my eyes I followed him. As I matched his steps, I thought to myself…

Oh, Jamaica you're going to be fun

We received our information on the flight, and boarded.

The Pilots greeted us, and we then began our routine.

Just as with the Italy flight…. The drinks, food and appetizers were

Spectacular!

We taxied down the runway and soon took off.

Ashton and I seemed to work in cinque. Everyone seemed happy and satisfied with our service.

The drinks flowed through out the flight. The best of the best wines…

And of course, exotic appetizers! They had requested an Italian menu, so the cabin was just filled with the aroma of tomato and cheese!

I`m always torn between Italian, and Chinese food myself.

We are given a meal as well… so it`s awesome! I had gnocchi, and Ashton chose Penne Primavera. It was to die for!

Soon… it was time to prepare for landing.

Chapter 10

Once we touched down, in Jamaica, we cleaned and waited for our Limo to our hotel. As soon as I step foot onto Jamaican soil, I felt the vibe. It was something unreal. That energy that I felt was unmatched.

It was like someone had plugged me onto a charging port and I was feeling the energy in my veins.

"This is beautiful" I said to Ashton who was just as in awe as I was. The street was colorful and brimming with people. The corners were loud and busy, the roads filled with yellow cabs racing by and commuters returning to their home, and people just enjoying life.

As we pull up to the hotel, I look around to admire the beauty that was on offer in the beautiful country of Jamaica.

"God, I didn't think this could get any better than this," I said in awe of the beauty of the hotel. 'I know right?" Ashton said as we checked in, gave our luggage to the bell boy and walked together down the wide hotel corridor, to a mezzanine floor where the elevator was.

The hallways were grandeur, and the interior matched the

vibe of Jamaica. It was lively and energetic. As the elevator came to our floor, Ashton and I entered together.

There was no one else inside beside us.

Should I say something to him?

My mind was paralyzed with apprehension. But before I could say something to him, his soft, warm voice startled me from a possible anxiety attack.

"What do you feel in the mood for dinner?"

Oh, an easy question for starters. "Anything that I can find on the hotel's menu." I shrugged my shoulders.

LOL Sophia. You don't come to a new country and eat basic food.

He wasn't entirely wrong.

"Well, in that case what are you thinking of, I posed the question to him.

"I am thinking to go out on the street and have a bit of street food,"

"Street food! that sounds appetizing, do you mind if I join you?" I said almost excitedly, and he nodded.

"Your floor's here Sophia," he said, and I looked up at the elevator screen.

"And to answer your question from earlier yes you can come with me. I was hoping you would.

I nodded and walked out of the elevator. I'll be ready in five minutes I winked and walked off to my room. As I reached the end of the corridor, I saw the bellhop waiting for me there. I dig into my purse and hand him a tip., I peek up at him as I stand waiting for him to unlock the room.

My room was honestly the most beautiful thing I had laid eyes on. It was spacious, it was modern, and it was exactly what I had dreamt of. But I didn't have time to fixate on the room. I had to be out in 4 minutes lol.

In the next few minutes both Ashton and I were on the streets of Montego Bay. Ashton seems to know exactly where we're going. We walk briskly up to the corner and onto the main road. Voila, this is the food we're going to have. He says as we stop in front of a truck. "This place has perfected the art of grilling yellow yam and I kid you not it's the best thing on this planet when you have it with saltfish."

"Okay Mr. if you say so, bring it on," He smirks at me and walks to the truck to order. In 4 minutes, he comes to me with two aluminum foils in his hands.

"Bon appetite," he says, and I glance around for a place to sit.

"Where do we sit?" I ask and he looks at the sidewalk. "The best seat in the house," I say okay, and I sit down beside him. As we start eating, I take the first bite as he looks at my face intently. I chew on the yam and his eyes are stuck on my face like he's waiting for my verdict. To throw him off I make a face, as if I didn't like it and I could see his beautiful face turning into a frown.

"This is extremely underwhelming…" I say and his face just droops even more. The moment I say that his face lights up. "I love it Ashton, now eat yours," I nudge, and he laughs. "God, I can't wait," he says as he takes the biggest bite.

As we both sit on the sidewalk, I realize that talking is just easier now, and it's easier than just being awkward and staying silent, and everything I say is the right thing and he nods and laughs.

By the time we get back to the hotel, I`m getting exhausted.

Let's call it a night, and maybe if you don`t have other plans, we can have breakfast and find something to do together?

Sounds great Ashton Sofia replies. How about 8.00 AM

It`s a date…...um I mean …sure good idea lol.

We both went to our rooms.

As I sat on the bed I took a long deep breath, it was so comfortable that I felt like I was sitting on a cloud. I took out my phone and I started scrolling on google to see places to visit. I find a few cool places to check out. So many beaches it would be nice to relax a little on this trip. Catch a nice tan to compliment my blonde hair. Do some reading maybe?

And of course, the one that's a constant in no matter where I am….SHOPPING!

As much as I was hoping to be with Kaylee… I am even more thrilled to be with Aston for some reason.

Hmm why am I suddenly thinking of him? Oh, maybe because he has a sweet smile or maybe it's because of the way he talks.

That thought brought a few butterflies to my stomach. I blink swiftly, my eyelids matching my heart rate. As the thoughts of Ashton infiltrated my mind, I laid on my bed. My heart started to beat a little faster and I don't even remember when amidst the crashing thoughts of Ashton and his smile.

His beautiful smile…I found myself in deep sleep.

Chapter 11

The next morning, as I woke up, I jumped out of bed. As I stretched my arms for a while, I went to the mini kitchen that was in the hotel room and made myself a cup of coffee. It was an Italian blend that I had picked up in Italy.

I took a sip as I breathed in the aroma of the coffee that transported me back to ROME.

Mumm. How delicious.

To enjoy the coffee more, I walk towards the balcony of the room. As I sipped the coffee, I felt myself getting sucked into more than just the coffee flavor. It was the thoughts of Ashton that were intruding once again.

But before I could clear my thoughts. they were broken by the sound of the phone ringing. RING RING, the sound echoed across the room. I walked in off the balcony and to the bedside where my phone was.

I answered only to be greeted by a very familiar voice that filled my stomach with butterflies. The voice was warm,

It was Ashton. I felt like I had been caught, but he couldn't possibly know I was thinking about him, right?

Unless…he could read minds.

"Hi Sophia," he said cheerily. Cleary he was passed the morning coffee phase and was clearly much more awake than I was.

"Hey Ashton,' I answered back My energy was WAY less compared to him.

"Why does it sound like you just woke up," he said, and I chuckled with embarrassment.

"Yes, I actually did just wake up,"

"Ahh well, I`ll be ready in about 5 minutes.

Yes, me too. See you in the hall.

We ventured down to the Hotel restaurant for breakfast.

Our food looked delicious.

We sat chatting and Ashton asked if I would like to spend the day with him. He made some suggestions, one including the beach!

He mentioned the things I had just thought of last night.

"What do you think? does any of this sound good? he

teased me, and I chuckled again.

"Yes, it does, especially the beach part,"

We finished our food and started for the exit.

"Perfect, see you in the lobby in the next twenty minutes. Wear a lot of sunscreens."

I quickly go to my room, and then spend a good ten minutes choosing a bathing suit. I slipped a comb in to keep my hair on one side of my face and applied just a little bit of mascara and some lip gloss.

I had done my subtle makeup, but I hadn`t picked out something to wear yet. I unpacked my suitcase and picked a mint green pair of shorts and tee shirt, that I had bought in Italy. It was perfect for the weather. I walked to the lobby, there was no one there. Patiently. I waited.

That's when I saw him enter the hallway. He stopped and was just staring at me.

He walks close to me with a finger across his lips. I think he was trying to suppress a smile.

'Sorry for staring," he said but you look amazing!

"You were staring? I didn`t notice?

I blinked at him, unsure what to say, and I think he could sense that, and said ...come on…lets hit the beach!

"Oh

"And I am sorry for making you wait, my card key wasn't working, and I had to wait for the front desk to issue me a new one, to get in my room, so I rushed…but I must say you're dressed for Jamaica," he says cheekily and I smile.

"Don't worry about it, I didn't have to wait long, 'and about the 'being dressed for Jamaica'" My lips quirk up in a sly smile well I am glad you think so,"

"Shall we go?" He smiles in response, and I nod.

"Let's go," I show him the way and the both of us walk out of the hotel to the car that was assigned to Ashton.

My mouth drops open.

It was a vintage red color Bentley.

"This is what you got?" I asked, my mouth still open in shock and he nodded.

"Well, we have our perks Miss Sophia," he winked at me

and opened the door to the car as he asked me to sit inside.

I quietly obeyed and sat inside.

Well, this was going to be fun! …

Ashton jumps in and we set out for the beach!

We sure turned heads …let me say!

Both of us with long hair flowing in the breeze.

While we were winding our way through the palm tree lined streets, we came upon a marketplace.

STOP! Sofia squealed. Let's check this out quickly!

Ashton pulled over into a parking spot. We`ll just skim through and see what's here. We can maybe come back another time.

The market had everything! Handmade bowls. And figurines, hats, dresses, fruit, and vegetables.

Ok…Lets carry on to the beach. It was just down the road. They found an empty spot and pulled in.

They grabbed their towels and more sunscreen,

They laid their towels out and walked towards the water.

The waves came up and Sofia felt the warmth on her feet. Ok… this is heavenly Sofia remarked as she began to splash Ashton.

HEY! I`ll get you back lol. Slowly they wondered deeper and deeper. Then… Sofia made her move and dove under. OMG… this is beautiful!

Ashton then did the same. He popped up and shook his head, and his hair sprayed Sofia. They splashed around for quite some time. Then got out to lay in the sun. After about an hour. Ashton mentioned they go on the Zipline, he had noticed when they entered the beach.Ohhhh I`m afraid of those Sofia shook her head. I`ve never been. It`s O K Sofi…. I`ll be with you. Sofia reluctantly said ok.

There was a young boy who was in charge. Ashton paid him, and the proceeded to get hooked up.

Sofia was scared, Ashton could tell. He assured her again it was safe…and they set her off. Sofia screamed all the way. Ashton followed and in seconds they were both on the ground.

I`m sorry if I forced you to do something you didn`t want to do. That was mean of me, I guess.

Nooooo I loved it! Thanks for making me.

Sofia Above The Clouds

Sorry if I acted like a baby.

Come on… lets head back to the hotel, we can change and have a drink and some appetizers at the pool.

Sounds great Sofia responds.

Back at the hotel, the found two chairs in the shade.

They each ordered a beer, and some snacks. That was

Wonderful wasn`t it? Yes, say's Ashton. I think we got a bit of color too.

They laid back and just enjoyed the scenery, and the people in the pool. They even fell asleep for a brief time. When they woke up… it was time to have a light dinner there at the hotel, and then, call it a day.

They were done lol.

They made their way back to their rooms and said good night. About an hour later… Ashton called Sofia and asked if they could have breakfast in the morning. Sofia agreed happily.

She soon fell fast asleep, and didn`t wake up until 7.00 o clock am. Wow... that was the best sleep yet!

She jumped up and into the shower. Next, she put on another

new pair of shorts and tee shirt. She made a coffee and sat outside. Morning Sofia, the voice came from a few balconies down.

Oh hey…you`re awake Sofia answers. Good morning!

How about a half an hour? Sure, Sofia responds. I`ll be ready.

They ate and headed out for some shopping. They went back to that market the had checked out briefly.

They had beat the crowds. That made shopping much easier. They both found a couple bathing suits…shorts, tees, and funky hats.

As they walked back to their car… Sofia stops suddenly. She spotted a small group of men just on the corner, in a huddle. She knew what that was.

A drug deal! Just as Ashton was about to ask what was wrong, one of the men turned, and saw them watching. Sofia shrieked and grabbed Ashtons hand……RUN!

Without looking, they crossed the road and ran into the high grasses and trees. It was like a jungle. Two of the men started after them. They soon ran out of the protective wooded area… and had to dash in and out of doorways down the street. The men kept on them.

Holy Shit Ashton yells in small breathes! What is happening!

Sofia said shut up and just run… I explain when I catch my breath and a break. We must lose those guys first. They come up to a small boutique and entered. Out of breath… Sofia asked if there was a back way out. The woman led them to it and the headed down the next street. They thought maybe they lost the guy`s… but no. Soon they came around the corner!

OMG…I think we`re dead. They kept on running and ducking in and out of doorways... but it was useless.

There was a field at the end of the street, and they headed for that. Bad mistake. Now they were out in the open and sitting ducks. Sofia fell to the ground, unable to run anymore. Sorry Ashton… it was nice knowing you!

Ashton was just in shock at what was happening.

The two men caught up to them.

Sofia held her breathe. Then started rambling.

We didn`t see anything…. we won't tell anyone anything we are just tourists Please let us go.

I didn`t see your face! My eyes are closed, see?

The main man, Smirked and told Sofia to stand up.

Hesitantly she did as she was asked. She began to cry.

Ashton moved over and took her into his arms.

What do you want with us he shouted!

The man covered his mouth and said stay quiet.

Sofia looks up just in time to see the man reach into his pocket, and she lets out a muffled scream.

Her eyes were now closed shut... in anticipation.

We`re going to die.

The man pulled out his hand....

There wasn`t a gun. There was a Badge!

These men were CIA!

Sofia and Ashton froze in shock! Their mouths just hung open.

Miss... what you saw... was a drug sting. You`re lucky it worked out ok.

We didn`t want you going to the police or news, that would destroy all our hard work.

The two finally let out a sigh of relief.

Wow… I`m just speechless! I thought we were going to be killed here!

I need to catch my breath a minute. Sofia took deep breathes. I haven`t run that fast and that far… since high school.

Me either Ashton lets out a deep breath.

We`re sorry this happened Mam. Are you going to be, ok?

Yes…. Yes, now I know what's going on.

An unmarked car pulls up to the beginning of the field. Here let me give you a ride back to your car.

Great … I can`t walk anymore now for a while lol.

As they drove…the man asked that they not repeat what they saw to anyone. It could hurt their case.

Sofia and Ashton quickly agreed. You have our word.

Thank s guys…and again I`m sorry for scaring you.

That`s ok… Thanks for the ride.

Ashton and Sofia drive back to their hotel.

Both were speechless.

They decided to have a drink, at the bar.

Well! That was a different kind of day…LOL

They both relaxed a bit.

Sooooo   Where shall we have dinner?

They broke out laughing.

Wow... THERE`S a story to tell when we get home!

Yaa... Who`s going to believe that.

Ashton was in the mood for some Jamaican beef Pies.

Sofia had never had them. Oh... you`ll love them. They are a bit spicey, but not too bad.

Ok great. They ordered right at the bar.

I thought… Ashton say`s, maybe we could go back, and take a moonlight stroll down the beach.

What do you think?

Sofia Above The Clouds

Sofia looks up and say`s. I think that would be very nice.

Sofia must have been famished. She was finished in no time. `
They were excellent Ashton. I`ll have them anytime!

Good I`m glad you liked them.

Let`s go.

The left the hotel…. The Bentley glistened under the lights of
the Resort. I feel like a movie star, riding in this car! Sofia
commented.

Ashton responds with…. I think you ARE a star.

Sofia blushed. The drove through the area…taking in the
sights. It was a balmy evening with gentle winds.

The reach the beach area and head down to the water.

The moonlight shone over the water creating sparkles and
glitter.

They put their feet into the water …which was now cooling off.
In silence, they slowly stroll absorbing the beauty.

I really needed this Ashton, Thank You.

Well…. Ashton speaks softly, I think we both needed this.

Sofia was getting tired at this point, and suggested they head back for an early night. Ashton agreed.

Yes…we`ve had quite a day. Maybe tomorrow if you`d like, we could go out and hit every shopping place around lol then take a long drive around the Island? Maybe discover some special places.

Sounds great Sofia smiles.

They reached their car… and drove back to the resort.

They said good-night and Ashton gave her a light kiss on the cheek.

Good night, Ashton. Sofia opens her door and disappears inside. Aston did the same.

Chapter 12

The next morning…Sofia woke up feeling refreshed and excited about their plans.

She was filled with butterflies, thinking of spending the day with Ashton. She jumped out of bed…and made a coffee. As she turned towards the bathroom…she noticed a paper, folded sticking through her door. She went over and pulled it out.

It read…………..

Morning Sofia! I hope you slept well. I am down at the little café by the pool. Whenever you are ready, you can meet me here. No rush…. I`m just enjoying the gorgeous morning.

Ashton.

Oh, perfect she thought. It won`t take me long to throw on my clothes and a touch of make- up.

She drank her coffee while she got ready…and with a splash of her new Italian perfume, she scurried down to meet him. More butterflies! She touches her stomach! Soo many butterflies!

She entered the café, and found Ashton, lost in thought, gazing out at the pool area, which was surrounded with the most heavenly gardens. The flowers were of the deepest colors of the rainbow!

There were fountains with flowing waters, and birds chirping in song.

Morning Ashton! He turned to see a bright-eyed Sofia smiling at him. I saved you a seat lol.

Oh… Thank You lol.

I had to download a ton of pix to make more room! Lol.

Yaa I did the same, Ashton laughs.

Let's order a light breakfast and make our way out.

Sounds great Sofia says.

The each had a coffee and took a walk around the pool. The waterfalls had such a mesmerizing affect, on them. This is a dream Sofia thought out loud.

They both had their phones out and were going crazy with pictures and selfies.

Yaa I could live here! Anytime.

Sofia Above The Clouds

Come on… there`s more to discover!

The made their way out to their car… which today was an SUV. Awesome Sofia say`s…. This is

Beautiful. I love SUV`S.

I was hoping you would, Ashton smiles.

It has a great GPS system built in, so we won`t get lost lol. Now, let's have a more relaxing, uneventful day. They both laughed!

Let`s start at that marketplace we sort of passed through. Now we can take our time.

Sure …Ashton replies.

They were able to park right up close and wandered in and around. Sofia found a nice black cape.

Wow… I always wanted a cape, and black is my color!

Ashton spotted a cool Tee shirt and cotton shorts.

Ok…… next?

Soon they were on the road and enjoying the drive.

The scenery was simply gorgeous. Oh, look Sofia points… a

waterfall! This would be perfect for a picnic! Great Ashton replies…. Let`s have one here

Yaa would be nice, Sofia pouted.

Noooo really…. I took it upon myself and had the hotel make us a fabulous Jamaican picnic.

He pulled over and went to the back of the SUV, where he lifted out a cooler style picnic basket.

Really? You`re kidding me…How did you manage that?

Ohhh I have my ways lol. Well awesome. You think of everything don`t you.

I try Ashton looked proud of himself.

Well, this is a treat, and I`m getting a bit hungry.

Thank You!

Oh! And they made you some of those Beef Pies too.

Wow You`re the best!

The food was amazing…just as the sounds of the water and the hot Jamaican sun. More selfies!

After a couple more hours, of driving and stopping at small little shops, they decide to head back, and chill around their hotel pool.

The next couple of days, they did the same.

Sightseeing, taking Pictures, and lounging around the pool and gardens. They ended there evenings with a wine and some snacks.

They felt more and comfortable with each other now.

This has been an amazing week Ashton…Sofia words faded out.

We only have about a day and a half before going back to New York. I`m so glad I was able to have you here. I thought Kaylee was fun…. But…...

Buuuuut? Ashton questioned? `

Ohhhh nothing. let`s have another beer.

Sofia was fighting off those butterflies again.

After their beer, they decided to take a break, and head to the rooms for a rest before dinner.

Sofia had spotted an Italian restaurant not far from the hotel.

Hmm how about we give it a try?

Sure… Let's say 6.00PM?

Sounds great Sofia agreed. I`ll have time to shower and wash the sand out of my hair lol.

Ok... I`ll buzz you just before Aston says.

Sofia fell fast asleep, from all the fresh air, sunshine, swimming, woke up refreshed.

She needed that break.

Soon, they were being seated in a cute very Italian eatery. The ambiance and aromas permeated their senses.

Sofia lets out a sigh. I feel like I`m back in Italy.

That must have been fabulous Ashton comments.

Yaa It really was.

Well……Cheers to Italy! They tap glasses. And…cheers to Jamaica!

They ordered and sipped a wine while waiting for their food.

I had an idea for our last day. Oh, Ok Sofia responded. What`s are you thinking?

How about… we go back to the beach, take in some rays, and then after a nice lunch, we treat ourselves to a luxurious afternoon at the spa!

Sofia`s eye light up. OMG That sounds wonderful!

Great Idea! Ok… Done.

I already booked us in for several treatments.

You did? Sofia laughs. She shakes her head.

I won`t even ask lol.

Cheers!

After dinner, they went for a long walk under the beaming moonlight and took in all the last of the Jamaican atmosphere before settling in for the night.

Montego Bay is just breathtaking!

So... How does 9.00 O clock sound for breakfast?

Our appointments are for 10.00.

Perfect Sofia agrees, and they say goodnight.

Again, Ashton gives her a kiss on the cheek.

Sofia is overwhelmed with butterflies as she looks at Ashton and again says goodnight.

Chapter 13

At breakfast ... Ashton went over the treatments he had chosen.

So …how do these sound….

First—a manicure. pedicure. And facial.

Then…They had a special on a couple's massage.

Soo I took it.

After that we have a Seaweed wrap.!

WOW…You`re really into the spa thing.

Sounds amazing!

Great I was hoping I chose right.

Can`t wait! Sofia beamed!

10.00 O Clock came…and they entered the most lavish serene atmosphere they had ever seen!

Tranquil music surrounded them, and crisp clean towels, a robe, and slippers. Ice water with citrus was there to enjoy.

I can`t imagine any place more heavenly! Sofia sighed.

Wow…I`m speechless Ashton replied.

They were each greeted by their private hosts and then taken off to their luxurious oasis.

The treatments played out over 4 hours. The last, ending with their massage.

They were both dopey and half asleep when the experience was over.

They thanked their hosts with an extra-large tip, and slowly headed back to the café.

OMG… I have never felt so wonderful!

I`m addicted! I think…Ashton says.

Don`t talk… just enjoy Sofia responds. Her eyes were half shut.

What a perfect way to end a trip! Thank You Ashton.

How about we meet back here around 7.00 for a light dinner, and swim. Then I think we should go to our rooms and pack. We have an 8.00 O clock flight.

Yaa that sound good. I know I`ll be sleeping deeply tonight!

Oh Yaa…Ashton nods. That`s for sure!

They head up to their rooms.

Sofia got comfortable and laid back on her bed.

She found a movie to watch and started to drift off.

After a brief rest. Her alarm went off. It was 6.00 PM.

A quick shower, make-up, and a casual sweat suit. She headed to the café.

Ashton was there waiting.

Hey… you look refreshed. Yaa, I feel great! How about you? Sofia inquires.

Well…....I`m good too.

SOOO. Ashton says. Have you checked your emails?

Not lately why?

There`s one from Exotic!   Oh? Sofia looks up inquisitively. What does it say?

Apparently, Kaylee was scheduled on a trip to Switzerland, but she is sick!

Oh, nooo hope she is O K?

Yaa… just a very bad cold, but not good if she`s coughing all over the guests! Lol

O K says Sofia, so what does mean?

Yaa so the trip is in TWO DAYS!

They are asking if we could fill in….and if we agree...

There would be a phenomenal bonus.

Oh wow…two days Sofia shrieks! Hmm.

I`d love to see Switzerland…… what about you?

It does sound very cool.

Ashton shrugged, then smiled. Let`s do it!

It`s only 5 days. Some super executives are going for some business meetings.

Well? O K.   Let's do it!

Cheers to Switzerland!!!!

Well…. I think, after a quick salad, and one glass of wine….
I`d better get started packing.

I`m going to need my beauty sleep now lol.

Me too! It`s going to be a very fast two days.

I`ll order us a couple of bagels and coffee in the morning to take to the airport. We can eat there.

Yes... that way, we can beat the traffic.

Their salads came, and it was delicious.

That was just perfect Sofia lets out a breath.

O k. what time should we meet?

How about 6.45 ...That way we have lots of time to get our instructions, then eat.

O k. I`ll meet you in the front lobby then.

Now… I`m going back up to pack, and then it`s lights out.

Good night, Ashton…... Good night, Sofia…. Sweet dreams.

The next morning went as planned. Soon they were aboard their plane, prepping for take-off.

Their guest were all nicely tanned, and touristy looking, for such an elite group.

The usual routine, went smooth, and they soon landed back in New York.

The guests thanked them for a wonderful trip. And left the plane. Sofia and Ashton quickly tidied up and headed into the airport.

Ok…we only have a day to get ready for Switzerland. I`ll call you tomorrow night with the information.

Great Sofia responded. Can`t wait!

Their taxis were waiting, and they drove off home.

The minute Sofia entered her apartment. She began calling her best friends.

She explained what came up…... and said they`d have to wait to get together after Switzerland.

They were a bit disappointed, but excited for her.

They wished her a great trip and would see her when she was back.

Next... check with Yvonne for another week of taking care of things. No problem. All set.

Good. Now to unpack, and then search through my wardrobe

for my winter clothes.

It's only really 3 days… if you consider the first and last is for travelling.

She chose her outfits… and found that with each item… her thoughts were of how she would look to Ashton!

She shook her head and carried on.

From there, she sorted her gifts for her friends, and set them aside. OK done. That was faster than she thought it would be.

She ordered her favorite Chinese food and had it delivered.

Tomorrow I will recheck what I packed... and have a day to myself. I'll look up Switzerland and see what they offer for activities…. other than skiing of course.

After she ate, she put on the T.V. and went out like a light. She never woke up till the next morning.

With the sound of her alarm, came the sound of rolling thunder! She slowly stirred and reached over to stop the ringing.

Ohh …It's raining! I love it! A perfect day to get over a bit of jet lag and have some downtime.

Tomorrow is a new adventure!

She jumped up and made the coffee. Aww fall is really in the air. Soon will come the snow.

Mmmm I really do love this Italian coffee. I should go online and see if I could order some lol.

I doubt it… but I could try anyway.

She changed from her night shirt, into her pajamas.

Then... she brought her big pillow from her bed, and a blanket.

She got cozy on the couch... and called Maina.

They had a long chat about nothing… Sofia wanted to tell her adventures when everyone was together.

That was becoming to be a ritual.

They soon hung up. Sofia found a nice movie.

Awww so relaxing. She drifted off and on throughout the day. Thoughts of going to Switzerland … and with Ashton, seemed to bring on those butterflies again.

Those butterflies grew even bigger, when her phone rang, and she heard Ashtons voice on the line.

Hey Sofia…. Are you ready for tomorrow?

Oh yes! I rested all day.

Great … so we are flying out at 11.00 Am. Not too bad.

Awesome. I`m ready to go now lol.

Can I pick you up? Ashton offers. Sofia agrees. That sounds great.

OK. I`ll be there around 10.15.

Perfect! I`ll be ready. Ok see you then, and they hang up.

SWITZERLAND

With the plane's ascent into the clouds my heart rose,

we were off to Switzerland.

In my mind's eye I saw the icy mountains climbing higher than I could fathom, and the pure white snow spread across the slopes. Ashton and I smiled at each other whenever we brushed shoulders in the plush cabin. I was in constant awe of the aircraft; its interior was of spectacular opulence.

Handing out menus, we tended to the needs of the ultra-rich, pouring some coffee, and others tea as they scanned the list of meals. The kitchen smelt divine as I went to and from serving dishes. I wish I was this organized at home, as this plane is.

About halfway there… the clouds slowly grew darker and darker. RAIN!

Fortunately, the turbulence was barely noticeable.

After an hour or so of no sun…the clouds dissipated

And the bright skies appeared again.

The captain's voice came on the PA announcing

Everyone to take their seats and prepare for arrival. Arrival.

After a smooth landing, we were at our gate of the Zurich Airport.

We assisted in their deplaning where they then went with their car services to their destination. By then I was dying to get off the plane.

We would soon be transported to our own location, St. Moritz, to the Carlton Hotel. There I planned to take in the extravagance that was Swiss accommodation.

I was blown away by the décor, the ambiance and royal welcoming. I shot Kaylee a text message. Sorry you couldn`t be here.

I will send all the pix I can.

We checked in without any delays and found our rooms.

The first thing in my sight, was the view overlooking the mountains!

The window was huge! You could see for miles!

I inhaled, taking in the beauty of the mountains! I turned to the bed sitting there invitingly.

Very German style. Soo different from Jamaica.

"Not just yet." I said shifting my gaze to the bathroom door.

I rested my hand on the exquisite handle and pushed inside.

 HEAVENLY!

Very modern, but with Swiss overtones. There was even a claw foot tub, with candles!

The counter was covered with all kinds of goodies, like soaps, creams, and even some Swiss Chocolates! OMG! Love this!

My phone rang... it was Ashton.

Hey! How about we go down to the restaurant, and grab a snack, and some hot chocolate!

There`s an outdoor patio with fireplaces and heaters!

OH, that sounds awesome! I`ll be ready in 15 minutes Sofia says excitedly.

Perfect Ashton replies. I`ll meet you in the hall.

Luckily coming from New York, they both had warm winter clothes!

They had no time to shop for any! LOL

Chapter 14

We were up and about early the next morning. We wasted no time exploring the splendid Hotel/Resort.

The first activity on my list was seeing the white mountains. The Swiss mountaineer train was glass-domed allowing a clear view of the picturesque scenery. The front desk ordered us a taxi. To take us to the Train Station.

This will be cool I said to Ashton! All Aboard! The man sang out.

We had our phones out snapping away as the train glided leisurely along its track.

The woman next to me, smiled and commented on the beauty.

"I've been to this unbelievably beautiful country three times now and its landscape still puts me in a trance. You're not alone. "I agreed Blinking to bring myself back to the moment and met her eyes. She smiled and shifted her gaze to the scenic Swiss Alps. "It's surreal!

The entire time we were traveling, Ashton was taking pictures. I think he hit every angle possible! Lol.

I spoke with the nice woman all along the way and back to

the station about the rich Swiss history, it's melting glaciers and wildlife that almost went completely extinct.

I think Ashton took enough pictures for us both!

The excursion ended and we were back in the heart of St. Moritz by late-morning just in time for lunch.

I`m getting hungry I hinted. Yaa me too Ashton Replied.

We decided on a small café only across from the hotel where the seats were outside amidst the bustle of the street and enjoyed the most appetizing meal while chatting.

Ashton suggested we try out the ski slopes. He`d like to take a lesson or two.

I think we had better! We`ll end up in the hospital, if we don`t! lol.

We'd have to sign up ahead of time for the next available lesson soon, because the sport was very popular among tourists. I called our hotel right then and got us set to go skiing just before the end of our trip there.

We toured the street side shops buying little things to take back home and stopping to talk with locals. Then we headed back to the hotel. We lazed around for the rest of the day enjoying the indoor pool and the people.

There was talk going on, about an evening party, out on the huge deck, the next night. Sounds awesome Sofia said excitedly! Soo we planned on it.

After a quiet dinner that night, we took a little walk in the area. The air was crisp and fresh.

O K…I think It`s time to go back, and maybe relax in our rooms. This cold is making me want to snuggle in bed and catch a movie.

I think you read my mind Sofia; Ashton agreed.

Munching on a piece of chocolate at 9PM, while cozy in my bed, in bed, an ad came on about the world's finest chocolates and I called Ashton... We both loved chocolate and we were in the home of the finest.

It was of course a must that we saw the Swiss Chocolate Factory. On our way to breakfast, we arranged for a tour. This could be dangerous you know. Sofia laughed. I hear Yaa responded Ashton.

Watching chocolate production firsthand and learning chocolate-making facts from veteran chocolatiers, we tasted the different treats on display. *Chocolate, chocolate, chocolate*, my mind went. The factory was some distance from the hotel, so we only did a short sightseeing venture. We wanted to be back for the evening.

With only being here a few days… we had to kind of rush through our wish list, but my excitement didn't dampen. I'd be waving Switzerland goodbye soon, but there`ll be another beautiful trip soon after.

Our experience here was memorable, I'm sure to be back some time and maybe again with Ashton!

We reached the hotel, and went to relax a short time, before getting ready for the evening party.

We entered the deck. There were fireplaces, all around. Each table had candles and dishes of appetizers. It looked dreamy!

We had to take pictures.

There was music playing, but at a volume where you could talk. We sat down and joined another couple.

The mentioned they were from Canada!

Oh nice Ashton replies. Then you must be used to the cold Eh!!! Lol

They all laughed. The gentleman said Awe … very good with our expression there. But…. no. Where we come from is usually moderate.

They talked for an hour or so…then Ashton asked Sofia to dance. A slow song was coming on.

Under the Swiss stars… their body`s moved in unison.

Sofia`s heart was racing! Ashton held her close, even after the song had ended. He tilted his head downward and gently gave her a kiss.

Sofia allowed it. She embraced it!

I hope I'm not stepping out of line. Ashton whispers.

Sofia shakes her heard shyly.

They sat down at the table.

"Here's to many more nights like this." Wherever we are! She held her glass to Ashtons.

"Cheers to that." And we drank.

The hours went by quickly; it was already twelve midnight. We told the couple good night and left for our rooms.

As they reached Sofia`s room. Ashton gave her another little kiss. She said good night and smiled before closing the door.

Chapter 15

They met up for breakfast as usual. Sofia was filled with those butterflies.

They ordered and enjoyed some coffee.

Well...Today is our last day!

We`ll try out the slopes, and maybe some last-minute shopping. What do you think? Ashton inquired.

That sounds perfect to me Sofia shivers.

It feels extra cold out lol.

Here Ashton gets up and places his sweater around her. I`m warm enough without it.

Oh... Thanks. I think my body is still a bit tired Lol.

Give me a few minutes… and I`ll be too hot!

You`ll get it back.

Ashton just waved. It looks better on you anyway.

Breakfast today, was more relaxed. They had lots of time before leaving for the ski slopes.

They discussed the trip. And had 2 or 3 coffees.

The view from where they sat, was like a postcard.

It was so easy to lose yourself within the mountains.

Ashton checked his phone for the time. O K... I guess we

should make our way to the lobby. The shuttle will be here very soon.

They got up and head that way.

There was a small group already there waiting.

In no time… they were on the shuttle and heading to the slopes.

On the way…Ashtons phone gave a beep.

He had an email.

He saw it was from Exotic Airlines, so he opened it.

It Read:

Halloo …. Switzerland!

Hope you`re having fun.

As promised, we have a bonus for you for helping us out.

We have a luxury Caribbean cruise for the two of you, on one of the largest ships in the world!

It`s for one week…with the option of staying on for another.

That`s up to you.

Again, Thank You for filling in.

When you return…we`ll have the details sent out to you.

Ashton closed his email. Without mentioning it to Sofia.

They reached the small hill area for their lessons.

(The Bunny Hill) The were given the equipment, and then a man came out to start the lessons.

Almost everyone fell, when they tried to copy the instructor!

It was a lot of fun.

They did manage to take a short trip down the hill finally.

They were not going to be attempting any regular sized hills on this trip, …so it was all in fun.

They built up quite an appetite out there.

When the lessons were done… they went with the group to the café inside the Ski resort.

Hot chocolates for everyone came first.

Mmmm! Best I`ve ever had in my life! Sofia gleamed.

I agree Ashton added.

They ordered a couple hot dogs. and sat with the others.

That was fun! What an experience!

We can say, we skied in Switzerland! Even if we sucked! LOLOL

No one will know anyway. Ashton starts to laugh.

At least!... Sofia shouts out…. We still have our arms and legs in the same places! LOL.

CHEERS!

Soon... the shuttle arrived back to get them.

The enjoyed their last views of the mountain in silence.

Back at the hotel. Ashton asked Sofia if she would like to join him for one last glass of wine, before they retired to their rooms.

She agreed.

Wow... that was so much fun! I`m so glad be did that.

Sofia`s eye twinkled.

You are right! I really enjoyed that too. Ashton raised his glass.

Here`s to maybe coming back another time! And I`m hoping it will be you...I come back with.

Sofia smiled and nodded.

Sounds wonderful... she tapped his glass.

They gazed in each other`s eyes.

Nothing was spoken.

Ashton broke the moment.

Soooo I received an email earlier from head office.

Remember they said they would have a nice bonus for us?

Yes... Sofia was hesitant.

Well... How does a Caribbean Cruise sound to you!

Sofia`s eyes widened!

What? Really! she screams.

Yaa…. Really! They are Awesome! I`ve been on a few. Ashtons adds.

OMG…I`ve always wanted to try one. Sofia gets excited.

When we get home… they`ll send the information, and we can see what kind of plans we can work out.

Wow…I can`t wait says Sofia.

Soo …. I think it`s time we call it a night.

Tomorrow it`s back to reality.

Yes, I think so Sofia pouts.

When we get home Sofia? Would it be OK if I call you?

Sofia looks up at him. I was hoping you would.

Ashtons face showed how happy he was.

Great!

As they left the café for their rooms, ... Ashton put his arm around her, and at the door, gave her a slightly warmer kiss, than usual.

Good night, Sofia…. We`ll meet up for a quick bite before heading to the airport.

How`s 6.00 AM?

O K…Good Night.

Sofia turned and entered her room.

She set her alarm for 4.30. Enough time to pack and

Sit with her coffee.

She jumped in the shower and then into bed.

In a moment…she was in a deep sleep.

Chapter 16

6.00 O clock came fast. There was a knock at her door.

Ashton decided to walk down with her to the lobby.

They checked out and headed to the airport.

Everything went great as usual.

The skies were clear, and the guests were in good spirits.

They felt even more like a team, since they shared

Those kisses.

It was a beautiful, unexpected whirlwind for Sofia.

Before they knew it... they were in New York.

The guests disembarked in a timely manner.

Sofia and Ashton did the same.

After their security check, the reached the outside of the

airport.

Can I give you a ride? Sofia.

She said that would be great.

Her eyes widened, as a Limousine pulled up, and a nice-

looking man got out and opened the door for them.

Sofia…this is Paul. They said hello. Nice to meet you Miss

Sofia. I`ve heard so much about you.

Sofia`s mouth dropped open. You Have?

Yes, said Paul with a wink…All good I assure you!

Sofia`s gaze turned to Ashton.

I`ll explain one day. Ashton gets in.

They drove her to her apartment, where Ashton got out, and gave her a kiss goodbye.

Can I still call you? He asks hesitantly!

Yes… call me tomorrow. I want to unwind tonight.

Oh Great…I will. Talk then.

Sofia headed up to her place. She dropped her suitcase and made a coffee.

I`ll call Kaylee…. Hope she`s feeling better.

Kaylee answered and sounded much better!

Hey…. You`re home she says.

Did you enjoy MY trip? Lol.

Sofia giggles …. Ohhhhhhhh Yaaaa!

Even more than I expected!

Ouuuuuuuu sound intriguing? Tell me more!

Sofia gave her a rundown of everything that happened.

Oh wow! Kaylee squealed. I`m so happy for you.

I had a feeling about how Ashton felt about you.

He used to ask me about you, but then… I didn`t think anything of it.

Now I know… he was interested in you more than he let on.

He really is an awesome guy, Sofia.

Well I hope things work out for the two of you.

Yaaa… I seem to really have fallen for him as well.

Soooo. We must get the group together in the next few days.

 I want to introduce Ashton to everyone.

I`ll ask him to join us.

Don`t mention it yet. Let me do it.

Sure, Kaylee states. Ohh I`m so excited.

Hey… Ricky and Fred might get jealous of him you know?

You are their favorite!

Noooo…They`ll be happy. They are like my brothers!

Yaa, I know… just kidding.

Ok…I`ll call them now. I`m glad you`re back.

Me too Kaylee.

I have some more news to share… but not till we`re all together.

Make sure Angel can make it too. I miss her.

Yaa I know. She works too much. I`ll threaten her LOLOL!

Ok…Whatever it takes. We all need to be together again soon.

Let me know, in the morning, so I can check with Ashton.

Got it Kaylee replied. Talk then.

Bye.

Sofia spent the rest of the evening, unpacking, and putting her gifts in their rightful bags.

This trip, she brought back Cheeses. and Chocolates.

They were made fresh from the source!...

SWITZERLAND

Sofia turned on her T.V. and gradually fell asleep.

Gone for the night.

Her cell phone alarm went off at 4.30 Am.

Dam…. I forgot to cancel that.

She rolled over and went back to sleep.

The sound of thunder woke her back up around 8.30.

That was about perfect.

She loves the rain, and thunder! Lightning she can do without!

She hit the button on the coffee maker and waited.

Soon, black gold was in her cup. Aww !

Delicious.

She no sooner took her first sip, when her phone rang.

It was Kaylee.

Ok… how is tomorrow. 7.00 Pm.

Sounds good to me Sofia replies. I`ll be talking to Ashton soon. Hope he is free.

Great. We`ll see you there

Sofia sat back and sipped her coffee. Her thoughts drifted to Ashton.

I`ve never felt this way for anyone before. I get butterflies and my heart just jumps.

I can`t wait for him to call.

The rain was really coming down hard now. She loved it.

She took out all her dirty clothes, to be washed.

Her new clothes she hung up.

She refilled her shampoo, and conditioner, replaced her toothpaste, and anything else she needed for her next trip. She loved her own products.

There were also some odds and ends, she always travelled with. A book, and her favorite late-night snacks.

Her phone rang. It was Ashton!

Well…. Hello! Ashtons voice flowed through her.

Hi…..How are you Sofia acted nonchalant.

She tried to hide her real feelings.

Did you have a good rest last night? He asked?

Oh yaa. I fell asleep early.

All that fresh air… was too much lol.

Like an overdose.

She then preceded to invite him out with her friends.

Ashton eagerly excepted. That sounds great he says.

Oh good. You`ll love them all. They`re all easy going.

You`ll love them.

Well… I`m looking forward to it.

Can I pick you up?   Sofia agrees.

Ok… I`ll be there around 6.45.

Awesome Sofia replies. I`m excited to see them all.

They shared some light small talk and hung up.

A new wave of butterflies fluttered in Sofia`s stomach.

She loves the feeling!

What should I wear tomorrow? I want to look my best.

She went to her closet, and started going through everything she had bought, in Italy.

Yes....She pulled out the sleek black dress pants, and one of the new blouses she had found.

Then she paired those with the beautiful silver chain and earrings she bought in one of those quaint boutiques.

Simple elegance.

She quickly put them on and checked herself out.

Perfect!

She made a call to her hair stylist, and begged to get in, either today or early tomorrow. Just a light trim, and shape.

It took some work, but with lots of fitness, she got in as a late appointment today.

Thank You…Thank You!

She wanted to look her best, for her friends, but even more so for Ashton!

The next day seemed to come in a blink!

Sofia flew out of bed, to the sound of birds chirping, and the sun. It is an exciting day. She had her shower and fluffed her hair. The trim looked amazing!

With her morning coffee, she started thinking about the Caribbean Cruise she and Ashton were offered!

She went on her computer and googled one of the large ships.

WOW! I had no idea they were this beautiful! I only thought of the Islands, when I did hear about them.

She started imagining herself and Ashton, enjoying the lavish amenities on board!

She closed her eyes, and was suddenly laying out by the pool, and soaking up the sun.

This made her sooo relaxed, that she fell asleep.

Chapter 17

The sound of her phone woke her. It was Ricardo!

Well… welcome home my dear! We missed you.

Ohhh hi sweety…. I missed you guys too.

Can`t wait till tonight.

Yes… I`ve got lots of hugs for you.

Ok…. well, we`ll see you tonight!

Talk soon.

Soon, Sofia, made a light lunch. Time was moving quickly.

She re checked out what she`ll be wearing and was satisfied.

She started putting on her make-up and playing with her hair. It was time to get dressed.

Her excitement grew.

I hope everyone like Ashton. I hope he likes them too.

All these thoughts raced through her mind.

The last step…. She chose an exotic perfume.

She was now ready!

Ashton called, and said he was there any time she was ready.

Ohhhh great I`ll be right down.

Sofia grabbed her purse and bag of gifts and headed out the door.

Lenora was just getting off the elevator as she got on.

Oh Hi! I can`t talk now… but how about tomorrow? Sofia said in a rush.

Sounds great…Have a good night, Lenora smiled.

Sofia exited the building, to find that Black limo waiting at the curb.

Paul was standing with the door open.

She stopped in her tracks. Hello, she nodded to Paul.

Ashtons head peeked out.

Good evening!

Sofia gets in.

She cleared her voice and turned to Ashton.

You Are going to explain this to me soon, right?

Ashton smiles…. Yes, soon.

A short drive brought them to the front doors of Alexanders.

Paul opened their door and said to just call when they are ready to be picked up.

Thank You they replied.

They entered and soon found Sofia's friends. They were near the back. Where there was a beautiful fireplace, and comfortable lounges.

Everyone stood up and greeted them.

Oh…and who might this be? Fred asked with an inquiring tone.

Everyone…. This is Ashton! I`ve been working with him. We were together for the Switzerland trip.

Glad to meet you! They all shook hands.

We had the most amazing time in the Alps!

Sorry Kaylee. LOL.

That`s O K Hun…. I forgive you. LOL

Hey Ashton… nice to see you again!

Kaylee smiled. Ya Same here!

Sit you two…Tell us all about your adventure!

Swiss Alps! That must have been an experience!

Fred stated.

Oh Yes… and they gave an overview of everything!

Oh …and here. Sofia reached down for her gift bag.

She handed them each a bag with their Swiss treats.

Maina spoke out.

We love her presents! LOL. She`s always soo   thoughtful!

Oh… It`s nothing. Makes me feel good to share with you guys. You`re all family to me.

Another round of drinks Ricky shouts out!

To best friends…. Family!

CHEERS!

Angel, stands and gives Sofia a hug.

I`m soo glad to have you as a friend!

I need all of you. My career becomes depressing after soo long. The hours are exhausting!

I know Hun…but you are so dedicated.

We need more nurses like you. You are special.

Thanks guys… I needed to hear that.

The evening went on. and then when it was time to leave, they all hugged.

Ashton was a big hit! They all had a blast.

Then they started with their escapades in Jamaica!

That was the big excitement trip!

They told the guys, all about the drug bust… and being chased.

The group sat intently listening!

OMG Sofia takes a big breath.

That was scary! The rest was…you know….

Sightseeing and SHOPPING!!!!! LOL

Anyway…That`s are brief recap.

Now I think I`m getting tired.

Time to call it a night.

We`ll be doing this again soon, I promised.

They all got up and made their way outside.

Ashton texted Paul, and he was there waiting.

Oh my! Fred says.

A limo Eh! Sofia? …I think he`s a keeper! Lol.

Sofia smiled shyly.

I`ll talk to you guys in a day or so.

 Good night!

On the way home…Ashton Thanked Sofia for the wonderful evening.

I`m glad you enjoyed my friends! They are special to me. I could tell that, Ashton adds.

Sooo …. Sofia changes the subject. Are you able to come over tomorrow?

Sure. What time? Ashton is happy she asked.

Oh... how about 1.00

Perfect! Can I bring anything?

Nooo..Just yourself.

Sounds good.

He gave Sofia a long, sweet kiss, and said good night.

Good night, she smiled.

Chapter 18

The next morning, she ran out quickly, to pick up some Kielbasa, olives, and bruschetta bread.

She`ll make a nice plate for the two of them.

He`ll be there soon, so she made a pot of her best Italian blend coffee.

Her doorbell rang and she let him in.

After a nice welcome, they took their seats at the table.

She poured the coffee and thought of the right words, to find out more of this mystery man Ashton.

As much as I`m glad to have you over...I do have an ulterior motive!

I figured you did Ashton laughed.

Maybe if I start first... it will be easier he states.

OH Ok...…Now fill me in on everything.

LOL..ok.

So... Firstly, I do have something I should have mentioned to you sooner.

The first time I met you... we worked together.

I just felt something special about you.

I wanted to get to know you better.

These funny feelings kept making me crazy!

Sooo I didn`t want to tell you who I was, until we got to know each other better.

Do you know my last name? he raised his eyebrows?

Sofia shook her head.

My name is Ashton Davis!

Sofia stared with a blank expression.

DAVIS! She looked puzzled.

You mean Davis as in Frank Davis????

Owner of Exotic Airlines?????

Are you related?

Ashton just nodded.

Sofia squinted and asked…. Are you, his son?

WoW…. Sofia sat in thought for a moment.

Sooooo That explains the Limo, and the Bentley in Jamaica.

Yes. Paul is my Private Chauffeur. He has been for years.

You know… Sofia slowly spoke while thinking.

I remember now. The first time we met… Kaylee did introduce you as Ashton Davis.

I guess it went right over my head.

Never would I have put that together!

Why didn't you just tell me!

Ashton apologized.

I didn't know how you would feel.

I've lost a few friends, because they didn't think they were in my class .

That hurt...I'm just a normal everyday guy....as you have seen.

I can't help who my parents are.

Soo I was afraid of you feeling intimidated too.

Are you upset now? He asked.

Sofia shook her head. No. And, I'm sorry you lost friends because of it. We need friends. `

Well... Thanks for telling me.

I haven't changed my feelings.

Ashton leaned over and hugged her tight.

Thank You.

I was just waiting for the right moment.

Sofia poured more coffee.

That Cruise we were offered...In my mind. I felt it was a bit lavish a bonus, for doing our jobs lol.

It all makes sense now.

Sofia Above The Clouds

O K!

Ashton Davis!..........

I`ll have to get used to that! Lol.

My boss's son. OMG.

So I`m afraid to ask. Ashton face showed concern.

But…have you thought at all about going on that cruise with me?

Sofia sipped her coffee and stared at the table.

After a few moments, she looked up and replied.

Well… I googled some major ships, and they were breath taking.

And…...I have always thought I`d like to try one day….

Yes…. Ashton awaits nervously.

Sofia smiles. Yes!!!! Let's go!!!!

Ashton jumped up and took her in his arms.

That`s awesome!!!!!! I was worried.

We`ll get the information soon.

Sofia sat down, and said:

Now I should tell you, my story.

Ashton nodded in response.

I lost my parents, when I was only three.

Ohhh so sorry!

It`s O k she continued. I barely remember them.

Afterwards. I was placed in foster homes. One after another.

It was the last one, who I had my first airplane ride.

With. They took me to Disney World in Florida.

Once I turned Sixteen. I had to leave foster care and make my own way in the world.

I was a waitress, and then also did some work at one of those annoying telemarketer places.

I remember falling in love with the plane.

I kind of decided then it was something I always wanted to do.

That`s what led me to be an Airline Hostess.

That pretty much sums up my life.

Not exactly like yours, right?

Ya you`re right Ashton says solemnly.

Well… I`m proud of you.

You`ve work hard for everything you`ve got.

You`re a strong woman.

Ashton pulls her close. He held her for what seemed an eternity!

Hey!! So let's start again!

Hello Sofia…. My name is Ashton Davis.

How are you! LOLOLOL

They both broke out.

Sooo We`re going on a Cruise!

And…. don`t worry… we`ll have our own rooms.

I`m not that kind of guy.

No expectations, No pressure….

I want us to take our time, and really get to know each other.

I`m soo glad you feel that way.

I`ve never fallen so fast for anyone before.

My career has been the only thing I concentrated on for the past few years.

This was soo unexpected.

Wow now it is starting to feel real!

We are going on a CRUISE!

Together!

They embrace…. ending with a long kiss!

Ok…. Sofia says.

I just got an email. Hang on.

They had me booked for FRANCE!

OMG.   That would be in 3 days.

Ashton made a frown.

How about after that trip?. I`ll really need a break by then.

 France …. Wow! How can you refuse!

Oh, Hey Ashton Perks up.

Maybe I can fix it, so we go together!

Sofia light up…. That would solve everything!

Ok… I`ll get on that right now.

He grabs his phone and calls head office.

They told him they would let him know in an hour.

Time seemed to drag on… Sofia poured more coffee.

Ashton started a nervous pace around the apartment.

Sofia just smiled with anticipation.

Ashtons phone rang….

Finally! He answers. Hey!... How did you make out?

Kyle was on the other end.

Good…It`s a go! You and Sofia will leave in three days for France!

Sofia Above The Clouds

O K Awesome! Ashton replies. You`re the best Kyle!

Thank You.

I`m here to please …You know I try my best.

 Have a great trip!

They hung up, and Ashton beamed.

It`s all set! We leave in three days.

OMG Sofia squealed! This is too much.

I need to shake my head. LOL

Soooooo….. I`ll have to do some more searching

For what to do and see.

Ohhh Ashton speaks up. We do know the main attractions,

like The Eiffel Tower?... The Louvre.

You know those places?

Oh yaaa!

French cuisine…Sofia adds…and SHOPPING! LOL

Ok… so I`ll check on the weather there, and pack for it.

I`m pretty sure it`s cool there now.

Sofia starts to think. Hmm. If we leave in three days...

That only gives us two days to prepare!

How about we go for an early dinner. And call it a day.

I have soo much to do!

That sounds like a plan... Ashton nods.

I would love some Chinese. That`s my all-time favorite! I could eat that every day. LOL

Sure.... I love that too!

Ashton taxed Paul...

They met at the curb.

Take us to the Best Chinese place in town!

You got it Paul replies.

They pull out.

They maneuvered their way through traffic, until the came upon Eastern Star.

The two got out and went inside.

Wow... They must have transported this place right from Asia! Sofia comments.

Lol. I think they did. Ashton adds.

They were escorted to their seats and given menus.

Sofia Above The Clouds

Everything sounds amazing! I`m torn on what to order. Ashton said not to worry.

The Server returned. and he ordered a variety of what he thought was best.

Perfect Sofia laughs. I don`t have to think.

Their food came in record time! Nice Sofia commented.
Smells like heaven!
 The food WAS delicious! They devoured it.
Wow… this was a great Idea.

I`m stuffed now Sofia sighs. That was wonderful.

I still can`t believe what is happening!
All these trips, and in such a short time.

The next two days will be a whirlwind.
I have a bunch of calls and explaining! LOL
Thank God, we`re still young!   She laughs.
Ashton agreed.

 Let`s get out of here and go back to my place.
One glass of wine…. Just one.
I`ll need to get a start in my closet! Lololol

After their wine… and discussion about Paris, Ashton headed out.

Good night, Sofia…. Talk to you tomorrow.

They kissed.

Ok…. Talk tomorrow.

Sofia got ready for a quiet night.

Chapter 19

The next day was filled with running around.

She connected with Yvonne, and apologized to Lenora, for not having time yet for coffee.

She went over her list again. and checked things off as she went along.

She needs a sweater, that will easily fit over her other tops.

She also could use a new pair of running shoes.

Those will have to wait till tomorrow.

The next day she just did what she could.

It was time to finish packing. Excitement was really setting in. They were leaving at 8.00 Am.

Ashton called. He said that he would be there at 5.15 to pick her up.

Ok ...should we pick up something to eat?

No, he said... I`ll bring us a coffee and bagel.

Oh perfect! That saves time.

It was an early night.

Sofia was all set for PARIS!

Again... she set her phone alarm, for the morning.

Soon she was fast asleep.

Ashton was there waiting, as he said.

Sofia climbed in the Limo, and they were off to the Airport.

Morning!... Morning.......

You look bright and cheery? Ashton says to her.

Well....... I feel wide awake and ready for Paris.

I spent a little time yesterday. Viewing things to do there

We can take a river boat ride as well!

Oh... that`s sounds good to me Ashton replies.

Paris at night sounds heavenly!

Yaa we`ll soon find out.

They reach the airport and say goodbye to Paul.

I`ll call you when we land in a week Ashton confirms.

You guys have a great trip!

Thanks!

They entered through the employee doors. Then with a

quick security scan, the headed to the plane.

They were the first to board.

Soon after the pilots arrive.

Both looked refreshed and ready to go.

Sofia whispers to Ashton…I`m always happy, when those guys look bright and alert. LOLOL

Just then… the guests begin to arrive.

Ashton and Sofia greeted them with smiles.

When the last was aboard, they closed the door and began their routine.

The engines roared and they began to taxi.

In moments they were heading into the sky.

The captain came on and announced that they were expecting a smooth flight.

The seatbelt lights went off. He gave their ETA and wished them a nice flight.

Sofia and Ashton then began serving coffee, tea, and a variety of juices.

With that, they also had an assortment of some of the finest pastries and bagels with cream cheese.

Wow… maybe we should have waited for breakfast Ashton whispers to Sofia.

She nods with eyebrows raised. Yes, I see!

And it smells like a French Bakery!

Love it!

While the guest enjoyed their breakfast… Sofia and Ashton had a few moments to relax, and chat.

Every trip they work… is a new experience and adventure.

They really enjoy working together as well.

There is no personality clash, like with some of the others.

That`s very important, especially when you`re are dealing with the very Elite!

You always must be in your Positive mode.

Once everyone had had enough food…

The made their way out, with mimosas.

Instead of champagne, they were made with one of the finest wines from France.

There was a nice-looking older gentleman, sitting on his own. He smiled at Sofia, as she handed him his drink.

Miss. I just have to say... I think you are such a beautiful young lady. You have a warm natural smile.

Aww Thank You sir Sofia blushes.

Are you into fashion at all? The man questions?

Ohhh yes, I love my clothes and shop everywhere I can. Well... the man lowers his voice.

A friend of mine…a very good friend, is in fashion design business in France.

He puts on a lot of runway shows.

If you`d like, I can contact him, and see if I can get you a backstage pass. I mean if your interested in something like that.

Sofia looked totally shocked!

OMG really? That would be amazing!

I`ll text him…and let you know when I hear back.

That`s if he has any going on this week mind you.

Wow…That would be the highlight of my trip!

Thank You so much!

She carried on with the service, then excitedly mentioned what he said to Ashton.

I hope he can get two passes.

Oh yes… I`ll ask him when he hears back.

It was about a half hour later, when the gentleman waved her over. Sofia approached him hopefully.

Well young lady…you`re in luck!

There`s a spring showing, in three days.

I have two backstage passes for you.

I didn`t think you would be going alone.

He gave me the address for you.

When you arrive. Just mention that you`re the guests of mine. My name is Marcell Lalonde.

His name is Antoine La Roche.

Ohh That`s is Awesomes. You're so nice!

How can I ever thank you?

No need… just enjoy yourself.

He just needs the names for Security.

They will have badges made up ahead of time.

Sofia gave her and Ashtons names and thanked him again.

Wow … this is unbelievable Sofia muffles her excitement.

I think I`ll have one of these Mimosas! LOL

She turned… facing the corner and tried a sip.

Wow…that is wonderful. The fine wine just took it up a notch.

Their didn`t seem to be as many drinking. Due to the time of day.

It was still morning.

That saved a lot of running back and forth on their feet.

The skies were blue…the sun was bright.

Time was going fast and soon they`ll be preparing to land.

They already had their prep area cleaned up.

What a relaxed flight it was.

Hey... Sofia says to Ashton. How about we stay close to our hotel for the first day.

We can check out our hotel. And enjoy where we are.

Over dinner, we can go over our plans, and sort out what order.

 I`ve had such a rushed, and hectic few days.

We have four days to explore.

Oh. And SHOP! LOL

Sounds fine to me. Ashton nods his head.

I`m easy.

The two got up, and started offering the guests their final drinks, and snacks.

There were only a few. They knew they`d be landing soon.

She thanked the gentleman again, as she passed his seat.

She and Ashton finished putting everything away and took their seats.

Ladies and gentlemen…the captain came on.

The seatbelt lights are now on. `

Please take your seats…we should be landing in 15 minutes.

Sofia glanced at Ashton. She was beaming with delight! Ashton reached over and took her hand.

PARIS

HERE WE COME!

PARIS!

As they landed... it was beginning to get dark.

There is a time change.

The lights looked beautiful as the sun went down.

They could already feel the vibe of French beauty.

The passengers began to exit, and the nice gentleman, winked at Sofia, and wished her a fabulous time.

She nodded and gave a grateful smile back.

When they were clear... the two of them did their clean up and passed through security.

With only 20 passengers. the prosses is very quick.

The Limo was there to take them to their hotel.

They pulled up to an amazing looking building!

It was almost museum like.

Holy Crepe! Sofia stares in surprise. LOL

This is unreal!

The entered the lobby, and checked in.

They received two rooms. Next to each other.

This is great! So nice to be close.

How about we unpack our suitcases, change, and just wander down and see if there's a café, or restaurant for a light dinner.

It`s evening here. We should try and stay on their time.

Makes things a lot easier.

I think you're right Ashton. Let's do that. I`m getting hungry anyway. Lunch... dinner…whatever! LOL.

Just give me a half an hour, I want to freshen up as well.

Sure, Ashton agrees. Sound good.

Sofia entered her room.

OMG… this is beautiful! So spacious!

There was all antique furniture, with mirrors, and brass fixtures.

Wow… this is a suite. Not a room.

The bathroom was huge! She stood there just admiring the

The work of art.

Quickly she showered and changed into a cute dressy sweat suit.

She headed into the hall, to meet Ashton.

Mmmm someone smells fresh!

Ohhh That would be me! Lolol they laugh.

They found one of the many places to eat in the hotel.

A small…charming café, that specializes in Crepes.

Ok… This is what I want… how about you? Sofia's eye light up.

Sound great Ashton replies. I love them.

The entered and found there were about a hundred different varieties!

Wow! This is cool!

Where do we begin! Lol

 Sofia reads the choices. Ummm I know what I`m having.

I`m trying the Coco crème, and the Bananas Foster!

Both with whipped cream.

Those sound awesome, but I`m going for…the Blueberry swirl, and the Apple cinnamon.

We can try each other's.

Oh yaa ..great!.

They ordered a coffee to go with that.

Let`s see how the French coffee compares to the Italian! Sofia states.

I know good coffee when I taste it. LOL

They found a table and waited for their order.

The sweet aroma of the crepes was intoxicating!

Now I`m really getting hungry Sofia says, with wide eyes.

It wasn`t long before their food came.

Looks yummy! Ashton lights up.

Here… let's take a piece of each.

Yaa!

The take their first bite.

OMG… I`m in heaven Sofia sighs!

These are the best Crepes I`ve ever had!

That`s for sure Ashton adds.

Wow!

Ok! I can have these every day!

Maybe we can work our way through the whole menu?

LOL.

Ashton sits back in a food coma.

He rolls his eye!

They decided to order two more.

Caramel Nut… and Champagne Dream.

They were just as addicting.

Ok…. We`d better stop at these. My clothes are going to

Be angry with me If we don`t lol Sofia remarks.

Well… I have my eyes on a few for the next time we come.

And…we WILL be coming back LOL

They praised the Chef, as let were leaving.

Let's take our coffee to go, and head out into the Courtyard.

Sounds good Ashton replies.

It`s still nice out.

We should try and walk off our food.

The courtyard was just a sight of beauty.

The floral design was like artwork.

Every plant was arranged in such flowing manor.

The colors were perfectly blended!

They came across a cozy antique looking bench and sat savoring their coffee.

This IS fabulous coffee by the way.

I`d say it was right up there in the top 5 lol.

Oh good…Ashton comments. God forbid it was just ordinary LOL

Sofia gives him a growly face! Lol

Shut Up!

Little by little, it grew cooler out. Sofia though it was time they went back up to their rooms for the night.

They could start fresh the next day.

Since they didn`t end up going over their list at dinner,
They would do that at breakfast.

They headed back in, and then said good night in the hall.
A warm embrace and kiss ended their day.

Sofia thought she would send some of the breathtaking
pictures to her friends. A bit of a tease you could say! Lol.
Mostly…she just wanted to talk to Maina and fill her in
about she and Ashton.
She also wanted to send Free. Some pix of their Crepes.
That was one of his favorites.

On the way to their hotel, she had spotted a magnificent
looking building. Then, as she looked further up …she noticed
it was a hospital!
It was like no other she`d ever seen!
It was absolutely gorgeous! She quickly snapped a couple
zoom pix for Angel.
Soon after, her eyes began to close.
There was just too much excitement for one day.
She got undressed, and into her night shirt.
In a matter of minutes, she was out like a light.

146

Chapter 20

The next morning, she awoke with the ring on her cell phone.

She looked at the clock, which read 8.00 AM.

Ashtons voice was on the other end.

Morning! He sang out. Did I wake you?

Just a little, she laughs.

Oh I`m sorry…I guess I`m just to excited to start our time here. Sofia laughed again.

Ok she says…. Give me 20 minutes, and I`ll be in the hall.

Great …. they hang up.

Guess what I want for breakfast Ashton raises his eyebrows!

Geee…. I don't know…CREPES!? LOL

Ashton laughs…. You`re sharp in the morning eh!

And…...that`s what they had.

Sofia ordered the Bacon, Maple…….and Ashton went with Honey Nut.

They were in heaven again!

Soo how about we make our way to the Louvre?

That`s where they filmed The Da Vinci Code.

That sounds good to me… Sofia replied.

They enjoyed their coffee for a bit, then called for a Taxi.

They really weren`t too far away, but the drive was still very scenic.

The Eiffel Tower was close there as well.

The reached their stop and thanked the driver.

He was nice enough to give them details of what they We're passing.

The atmosphere was in high gear. Tourists were all over the area. They made their way inside.

WOW…. I had no idea Sofia said in amazement.

Yaa…. Me either!

Both had opens mouths as they glanced over the walls of paintings.

I had no idea it was like this/ Sofia was in shock!

This is beyond words.

They slowly made their way, following the other tourists.

The ambiance carried them off to another point in time.

There was little to no speaking.

There were no words!

They were there at least 3 or 4 hours... lost in the works of art.

It must have been a very religious era back then.

Where did these people develop the skills?

Look at the ceilings! Wow!

How did they do that?

The walls are completely covered!

There was just one piece after another for what seemed like miles!

When they reached the end…they left with complete wonderment on the faces.

What an experience that was.

You know…says Sofia, I had heard of the Louvre, many times…. But never really knew what it was all about.

I`m sooo glad we came!

Hey… there`s a little café across the street. Let's take a break, and maybe enjoy some people watching.

Sure…. Sofia jumps at the idea.

I`m getting thirsty, and I love watching people! Lol.

They managed to get a nice bistro table by the sidewalk.

They ordered. Coffee and Croissants.

The sat back and went over the highlights of the Louvre.

That will be in my memories for a lifetime. Sofia lets out a sigh.

Can you imagine living the way they did?

No… I just felt so small in there lol Ashton replies.

While sitting there, of course Sofia noticed a couple small boutiques just down the street.

Hey... let's take a walk and see what's here.

Maybe some souvenirs?

Sure…Ashton agreed.

They finished their coffee and turned down the street.

When they entered this nice small boutique. They were warmly greeted.

It had soo much to look at. Clothes, toys, and replicas of the Eiffel Tower and other main attractions.

These would make the perfect gift for her friends Sofia thought.

They were not too big, so easy to fit in her suitcase.

Perfect.

She also chose a few nice scarves for the girls.

Who doesn`t love fashion? LOL

Ok…. Let's go back to the hotel.

My feet are getting tired. Maybe we should hunt for the gym…

We`d better work off all those Crepes.

And…...lol… make room for more!

You read my mind Sofia. Let go!

That was awesome She said as they gazed out the windows

of the cab.

We`ll check at the hotel desk for a gym, and, also, a spa.

I`m sure that luxury resort has something?

You would think so, Ashton replies.

The entrance to the hotel/ resort, was elegant, and pristine.

Every feature was immaculate!

Lights were woven all throughout the property.

Parisian statues lit up brightly.

Just spectacular!

They entered and approached the front desk.

There were many brochures to take, so they did.

Sofia took some extras to add to her bag of goodies for her

friends'.

They would dye to see this place.

They found their little café and sat going over the booklets.

Sure enough…there was a beautiful pool, and Spa.

Oh good. Ashton gets excited.

Let's call and make an appointment for after dinner.

The number is right underneath the name.

Le Spa Du Paris

Ouu sounds exotic.

Yes…. I love it!

Ashton called the number, and booked in for a massage,
and manicure for the two of them.

That`s perfect he says on the phone. We`ll be there.

He hangs up. Ok…. We are set.

7.00Pm. Maybe we can take a short swim just before.

And…. I think I`ll stick to salad tonight as well.

Good Idea Sofia nods.

They both went back to their rooms for a bit of a rest.

Sofia took a few minutes to organize her gifts.

Then she laid back on the bed with a book she had.

She enjoyed reading when she had the chance.

Ashton called; it was getting to be time to go for dinner.

They wanted time after that for a swim. Before the Spa.

This time… they moved quickly by the Crepe café. LOL
NO CREPES TODAY!

They headed to another little eatery, where it catered to

healthy eating.

This hotel/resort has something for everyone.

We had the soup and salad. Delicious!

A quick swim… and the……… SPA!

We entered, into the most luxurious Spa, I`ve ever seen!

The décor was of Parisian Flare at its finest

Two ladies greeted us, and we began our Zen time.

Every area we came to was dreamier the one before.

It started with a massage… then, a seaweed wrap.

While I laid there, the woman was giving my hair. their

Royal moisturizing treatment.

While she left that in…she then did the same on my face.

The aroma was pure indulgence.

The gentle soothing music brought me into another realm.

It was three hours of heaven.

To end the experience, a shower, with a spearmint mist.

I think that was to help you come back from your sleepy

daze lol.

Ashton was ready as I came out dressed and rejuvenated.

Shall we go for a quick coffee? He asked.

Sounds good.

I know it`s late…but I`m thirsty.

After reliving that experience, we discussed the next day

Events.

SHOPPING!

Then, SHOPPING!   LOL

We`ll have to be back though in time for the Runway Show!

Maybe we can video some of it.

I know, my friends will not believe me, when I tell them

about it! LOL

Ashton laughs…. would you? Lol

Probably not! Sofia replied.

O k…how`s this…...

A light breakfast, Then, we find one of the major shopping

areas, with your designer shops.

I know you`ve been dying to go!

Afterwards, we come back, and rest, refresh, and refuel,

before the show… Ashton suggests.

Perfect Sofia agrees.

Done

Here`s to our final day in PARIS!

155

Ok I`m done in now. Let's head up and get a good night's sleep.

I`m ready Sofia exclaims.

They stop at Sofia`s door, and after a short kiss, they say good night.

Both fell into a deep sleep.

Chapter 21

The next morning, the awoke feeling both excited, and Sad.

The excitement of shopping in Paris…AND a real runway show, but …it is their last day.

While savoring their morning coffee, Ashton reminds Sofia of their plans.

Yaa like he really need to. LOL

Sofia tells him she`s on a mission, for a few things.

An Exotic French Perfume… for one!

An authentic French suit for another.

Then. another trinket to bring home.

Well…Ashton replies, That you shall.
I know you will.

They went over to the concierge and inquired about the best places to go.

With that… he hailed a Taxi, and they were on their way.

On the way... they took some of their last pictures, of important places, that they passed.

In France, it`s never ending.

Ok…This is It!

We`re here.   Avenue des Champs-Elysees

Enjoy!

They Thank him with a nice tip.
 Wow…where do we begin!

Sofia spotted a real quaint boutique across the street.
They started there.
She found her Channel #5. Ahhhhhhh   Love it!
 I`m Happy.

Next… a few doors down, she saw another, advertising
Gucci bags!
They went in and wandered around.
They were soo beautiful.
They had a big sale happening!
She found two she loved and made her purchase.

Sofia Above The Clouds

Ashton just followed behind. There was just soo much to see.

She could have spent hours in each place.

He decided he would be the bag carrier.

This way. Sofia could shop easier.

When Sofia came across a little store, with designer brand outfits, her eyes beamed.

Ok here we are.

Ashton suggested she go in… and he would wait outside.

She said that's fine.

He had an ulterior motive.

Just a door down, there was a high-end jeweler.

He knew he would have enough of time.

Sofia disappeared and Ashton snuck into the jewelers.

He wanted to surprise her with a beautiful Tennis bracelet, if he could find one.

He went in and asked the woman behind a long display case.

She guided him to the bracelets.

They had quite a selection.

Soo many beautiful pieces to choose from.

Finally, he made his choice… A delicate silver with a hint

of black outline.

It was stunning.

He felt excited and asked the woman to gift wrap it for him.

He chose a black and silver box to match.

He was soo pleased with his choice.

Quickly he hid the gift in an inside pocket of his jacket.

She`ll never see it there.

He went back out to the sidewalk, as if nothing happened.

Sofia soon showed up, with a few more bags.

Ok… she says in exasperation.

I`m done.

Ok says Ashton.

Guess what I see. He teased her.

I don`t know? what!

There`s a Crepe Street truck just around the corner!

Let`s try it!

OMG nooooo lol Sofia fights the urge.

She sighs. O K. One last Crepe!

They chose…. Coco Caramel… and Strawberry Parfait.

Their last indulgence in Paris!

Amazing!

Maybe we should open a street truck like this in New York!

Maybe then we would get tired of them LOL

Never happen! Ashton groans.

Ok let's walk these off.

From there. they strolled down the busy street, taking in the sights and sounds.

It was time to go back to hotel and enjoy their last afternoon.

The Runway show was at 7. 00 Pm...and they had no Idea what time it would end.

It might ne a good idea to pack as much as they could.

They have a 9.00AM flight home.

The waved over a Taxi…and made their way to the hotel.

They struggled a bit with all Sofia`s bags and packages.

But. They made it. Lol

Sofia had to re arrange all her gifts again!

It wasn`t that bad, since they fly on a Private Jet…

The rules are different, as far as how many and size.

Wheeeew! Sofia sighs, as she closes her carry on.

She designated that basically for all her extras.

She had most everything packed now, but what she`d wear

tonight, and her uniform for the morning.

Great!

She jumped in the shower and started to get ready.

She chose one of her new Paris outfits.

A black and grey plaid mini skirt, with a sleek black blouse.

She had also purchased silver high heels, which had a delicate spray of sparkles.

I must admit… I do look awesome in this new suit!

She decided to wear her hair down, in a lose kind of

Messy style.

It really looked rather SEXY!

Next… she applied her makeup.

She went very light.

Black eyeliner…and soft pink lipstick.

To finish everything off……She put on her

Channel # 5 Perfume.

Voila!

Sofia was ready for the World!!!!!

She stood gazing at herself in the mirror, as she called Ashton.

Sofia Above The Clouds

He announced that he`d be outside her door in 5 minutes.

Great she says smiling at herself.

The excitement was kicking in heavy now.

A Paris Runway Show.

Wow!

Sofia stepped out into the hall and found Ashton waiting.

His eyes grew wide…and his mouth dropped open!

OMG… You are absolutely Beautiful!

Thank You Ash…. You look very handsome yourself!

What is that Perfume you`re wearing?

He leans over and gets closer.

This is one of my favorite scents.

Chanell # 5

Wow… it`s just beautiful!

Shall we? Ashton places him arm through hers.

I`m soo excited Sofia states, with a whispery voice.

Come on. let`s take some selfies, in the lobby, and by the gardens.

Arm in Arm, they pretty much floated down to where they could take some fabulous pictures.

They were a gorgeous couple.

Ashton soon removes the paper from the man on the plane, with the address to where the show was.

Sofia was about to call a Taxi... but Ashton tells her not to.

Why? She says looking puzzled.

There is a Limo waiting outside for us.

OMG! Now I really feel like a princess.

Ashton mouthed the words You Are.

There was wine to sip at ...while the enjoyed the ride.

Cheers to a wonderful evening .... Our Last in Paris.

Cheers!

The limo pulled up... and the gentleman opened their door.

There were people, and cameras, and lights flashing all around.

The excitement sent waves of chills through them.

Once they reached security. They gave their names... as well as the guest who arranged this.

With a huge smile, and nod...the man found their badges, and pointed where to go.

Another woman greeted them, and walked them to a huge warehouse type room, where there was a hustle and bustle of half-dressed young models, and hair stylists, wardrobe and makeup artists!

The energy was off the charts!

The woman walked over to a man... who was reading off some sheets of paper and yelling out demands.

He glanced over at them, and then the woman left.

He waved them over.

Hi... I was expecting you. I`m Antoine Sorry I can`t talk now.

There`s a table and chairs over there, and he points.

Just have a seat and watch the chaos! He laughs.

Ohhh my...... You are a delicious looking thing! He eyes Sofia up and down. Then peers at Ashton!

You my friend... I could just devour! LOLOL

Ashton blushes. Sorry, I`m spoken for lol.

They all laugh.

The two went over and sat down.

It was fascinating to watch.

Everyone seemed in a rush, and stumbling around for their accessories, hair pieces etc.

There was loud talking... and pouty models.

This is too tight......

I hate this color!..........

Sofia held off from laughing.

In the far corner... The Designer they met was yelling ..Cloe!

Where`s Cloe!   She should be here by now!

Some swearing ensued.

She`s my SHOW STOPPER!

Some one call her now please!

She`s always late!

One of the models, got on her phone.

Hey!.Where are you?

It`s soo late!

OMG noooo the young girl screamed.

She`s across town, caught in traffic!

Antoine started screaming for another model.

There wasn`t any.

OMG I`m ruined he shouted!

He started making calls. But there wasn`t time to bring anyone else in now.

He stopped in his tracks. He turned towards Sofia.

Hey…. Beautiful lady...have you ever modeled?

Sofia Above The Clouds

Who? Me? Sofia looks shocked.

OH No…she shakes her head nervously.

Please… come here. Antoine beckoned.

It`s easy! You just walk out… stop. They applaud.

Then… just slowly walk to the end of the runway and stop!

Then… turn around and back to the first stop.

Please!!!!! Can you help me out?

Sofia glanced at Ashton.

He nodded. You`ll be fine he said.

You`re a natural.

Reluctantly… Sofia agrees.

Fabulous!   Thank You.

Now hurry…. Get this woman ready. He shouted!

It was a whirlwind of makeup hair, and shoes.

Then… they brought out the Star design.

 The wedding Gown!

Sofia`s eyes light up with amazement.

The wardrobe crew had her in the dress, and it fit perfect!

Thank God……. lol

It was a bit snug, but no one should notice.

The Show began!

Antoine went out and made his comments.

Then... the music played.

One after another the models walked the runway.

The was a lot of loud applause.

Then silence.

Sofia was given her cue.

This is it!

She froze for a moment!... she couldn`t move.

The group around her encouraged her, and calmed her down.

In a matter of moments.......

Sofia on the Runway!

She stood poised, and the room Gave a standing ovation.

The dress was more than breathtaking!

She also was glowing under the lights.

She managed a slight smile and walked the runway!

When she found her spot... there was another roar of applause!

Flashes went off all over the room.

The other models now joined her, and then Antoine came out for his finally.

He thanked everyone for coming and for their support.
The room was filled with such joy, and emotions.
They lined up and took their bows.
Antoine hugged each model… and they
Made their exit off stage!

Ashton was there to meet Sofia… who was now in tears.
What just happened she shrieked!
OMG!!!!!!!!!

Ashton wrapped his arms around her. She was in tears.
They were Happy tears…mostly from shock! Lol

Ashton had gone out into the crowd when the show started.
He had taken some amazing pictures of Sofia.
 He was able to take a short video as well, as she walked the runway.
He knew, her friends would never believe this.
They themselves couldn`t lol

The wardrobe crew started undressing Sofia.

They brought over her suit, and shoes.

She was back out in no time.

You were awesome! Ashton said again.

That dress was made for you.

And…. you never even stumbled lol

Sofia   broke   out   laughing.

That's all I thought about she replies.

She let out a huge breath!

That was beyond, shocking.

I`ll never forget this night!   Ever!!!!!!

Now I guess we should go…

We have an flight in the morning.

They turned…. And a voice yelled out!

Sofia… Wait!

I can`t thank you enough for saving me tonight.

This is the busiest time for Fashion Showings…the models

are in high demand, and hard to find.

You were remarkable out there!

Sofia Above The Clouds

No one could have worn my prized Show Stopper, the way you did.

 Would you like to keep the Dress?

I really want you to.

Sofia almost fainted.

Really?

Antoine motioned for someone to bring the dress.

Yes…. You deserve it.

You gave it life… and everyone is sending out pix on Instagram…and Twitter…

The show was a smash hit!

So…. Take it… if only for a souvenir of tonight.

It belongs with you.

Sofia excepted the gift… and thanked him up and down.

It was a pleasure to meet you Ashton says.

Maybe we`ll see you again someday.

They turned and left the building, to their awaiting Limo.

I`m still shaking Sofia reaches for a glass of wine.

It doesn`t seem real!

OMG

I just wore an authentic Parisian Designer Gown.

Ok…let`s just sit in peace and quiet… I need to come down off this high lol.

The soon were back and headed straight to their rooms.

You were beautiful tonight, Sofia.

Ashton leaned over a gave her a kiss on the cheek.

It`s late. Have a good sleep, and I`ll call in the morning. `

I will thank you. You too.

She opened the door and went inside.

She hung up the gown, which was in a heavy plastic bag.

 She had a quick shower to save time in the morning.

When her head hit the pillow…. she was gone.

Chapter 22

The morning came too soon……...

But She was getting excited to get back to New York.

Ashton called, and they agreed on meeting in 20 minutes.

Sofia fluffed her hair and applied some makeup.

Quickly she packed what was left… and set her bags at the door.

With one last look at her room, she met up with Ashton in the hall.

They went down to the café and had a coffee and a bagel.

Sofia asked for the strongest blend they had.

Ashton just grinned.

I think we can both use that lol.

They drank up and check out.

They called for their ride to the airport.

Sofia was still a bit tired. She yawned.

We`ll be home soon… Ashton assures her. You can sleep all day tomorrow.

Ohhhh Yes, she yawned again.

It was overcast and with a touch of rain.

When they arrived and left the Limo…. they stood outside under the covering… which helped Sofia wake up.

Ok she says… I`m as good as I`m going to get.

Let's go in.

The passed through security…and boarded the plane.

First thing…...make the coffee.

They turned on the ovens and made ice for the juices.

The Pilots then arrived.

Good morning!

Good morning.

It doesn`t look like it now… but we should have a great flight home.

We`ll have the wind at our backs. Should be quick.

Sofia was elated.

The guests began to board. They all looked awake.

Soon they were settled in… and Sofia and Ashton began their routine.

The engines fired….and they taxied down the runway.

They had their last looks out over France.

Sofia whispered goodbye.

The seat belt lights turned off…. And the duo, jumped up and began service.

Fine French coffee, bagels, croissants, and mouthwatering pastries.

Diet food Right? Lol

Sofia approached the guest who gave her the Runway passes.

Good morning Mr. La Londe…

She thanked him again…and gave a quick description of their night. An experience she`ll never forget.

He was very pleased it was that nice for her.

No probable my dear.

It was my Pleasure!

Most of the guest seemed to fall asleep after their breakfast, giving Sofia and Ashton a break.

An hour and a half or so… more exquisite food was served.

Afterwards. Sofia and Ashton had a meal as well.

It was fabulous.

Time passed… and soon they were preparing for landing.

Both were tired.

They touched down… and the passengers left the plane.

Ahhh Sofia sighed. What a trip!

Well… I think you should stay in and catch up on your rest Ashton stated.

Maybe I can call you tomorrow?

Yaa that sound like a plan. A great plan lol.

Paul was there waiting, and they dropped Sofia off home.

Ashton helped her with all her bags.

At her apt. door, he gave her a nice kiss and smiled.

I`ll call you in the morning.

Ok… Talk to you soon.

Thank You.

Sofia dropped all her bags on the floor… except the gown, which she hung up.

She was exhausted… after such an overwhelming trip.

Normally she would have been on the phone to Maina…

But she just wanted to relax, and not have to get into any long conversations yet. Lol

She slipped into something more comfortable and headed for the couch.

Despite loving Paris…it was nice to be home.

She had no idea, what was going on in New York… since before Jamaica.

Everything just came up so fast, with no down time.

She got up and poured a coffee. She turned on her T.V. and sat back.

After 2 hours of news, on different channels, she felt she was caught up.

Nothing overly exciting or new. LOL

She changed over to a movie channel and found one of her favorites playing. She never saw much… her eyes grew heavy, and she fell fast asleep.

Between the jet lag. and excitement lag lol…… Sofia was done, for the day!

It wasn't until 4.30… that she woke up and felt some energy back.

It seemed kind of dark out already.

There was a bit of a storm coming in. The sky was grey… and she could see it was starting to rain.

OH Yaa…. Love it she talks to herself. It makes it feel so cozy inside.

She made another coffee, and went to the balcony door, to watch the rain.

She was coming back to normal, now she felt.

Her thoughts were getting clearer, and she had some newfound energy.

What a nice relaxing day… I need this.

She finished her coffee, and went to the doorway area, where she had dropped all her luggage and bags.

She gathered up all her souvenirs and placed them on the table.

While she was in one of the boutiques in France, she had asked the woman at the counter, if she could purchase some empty bags with their beautiful logo on them.

The kindly older woman handed her a bunch no charge. Sofia was delighted and gave her a nice tip.

They were soo perfect in size and were beautifully decorated with very Parisian style. Design pictures on them.

A souvenir in itself.

She lined them up… and had fun placing each trinket inside.

Then…. She opened her suitcase where she found the bottles of wine.

She placed a bottle in front of each bag.

What awesome gifts she thought to herself.

Just then…her phone rang. It startled her.

Maina`s …. voice was loud.

You`re home...she screamed out.

Yes…....I`m home.

How was Paris? How is Ashton!

Sofia laughs.

Maina… there is soo much to tell. I`ll fill you in, when we get together.

OH OK. Maina pouts.

I`m glad you are back safe and sound.

I miss you!

Can you just tell me one thing?... Main begs.

Ok shoot.

How are you and Ashton doing? Is there hope of something real?

Sofia paused…. I think there is Hun. We`ve had the time

of our lives… and he`s been such a gentleman.

I really have fallen for him bad.

I just want to take it slow though.

I want to be sure.

Oh that`s awesome Maina says.

Maybe he knows someone like him… for me too.

LOL

You know what i`m doing right now?   Sofia teases.

What!

I`m just getting your little gifts together. Lol

Ohh I love the sound of that! From Paris!

Just give me a day or so, to get organized here... and we`ll get together with the group.

The time change, and jet lag, are hard enough… but our last night, took it to new heights.

That sounds great! The guy`s will be happy to see you.

I`ll send you a few pictures, and the rest I`ll show when we`re together.

You won`t believe how our trip ended if I just tell you. LOL

Aww …. Now you have me crazy…Can`t you just tell me?

Nooooo!!!! LOL

Ok…I hate you!!!! LOL

They both laughed.

Ok.. I`ll call you. When I`m settled and refreshed.

We`ll decide then, what we`ll do.

Ok great Maina agrees.

Get some rest, and I`ll talk to you later.

I will.

See ya later… bye.

They hung up… and her phone rang again.

It was Ashton!

Heyyyy How are you?

Hi Ashton… I`m finally starting to feel some energy again LOL

That trip did me in.! I`m slowly getting unpacked, and my gifts sorted, and caught up with New York life. OL

I was just talking to Maina. We will find a day, to get together.

I hope you`ll join us?

Oh yaa for sure. Ashton lights up.

I really enjoyed meeting your friends! I`m hoping they`ll come to like me as well.

Well…. I already know they do.

Maina and Angel thought you were soo handsome!...

Ricky and Fred …. Well, they found you to be a real keeper…. LOL.

They always look out for me. They are my only family as you know my story.

That`s so nice to hear Sofia… You know how I feel about you.

Thanks for telling me that.

I really want them to except me too.

Those butterflies started to flutter inside Sofia.

They will…

Would you like to come by for coffee in the morning She asks?

That would be great Ashton sounds excited.

That will give me another night of rest. I should be back to normal by then! LOL

Ok. I`ll call you around 9.00.

I`ll pick up some croissants on the way.

Ohhh nice. I`ll have coffee ready.

I`ll talk to you then!

It`s a date Ashton replies.

They hung up.

Sofia went and unpacked the rest of her suitcases.

She hung up the new clothes she purchased, in Paris.

Hmm…. I really am going to have to do something soon,
For space. LOL

I could stop Shopping…...But that`s not going to happen!
LOLOL

Perhaps I should just pick up a separate wardrobe.

Yaa… that sounds better.

What was I thinking.... LOL

She took her empty luggage... and placed them under her
bed.

She was now on a well needed break.

After a light meal… she decided to watch, or try to watch,
a movie in her bedroom.

That way she would fall asleep early, just for the extra rest.

Ashtons smile, took over her thoughts, as she got under her
puffy duvet, and settled in. The cruise was on her mind as well.
That did sound exciting!.

And as expected… she was soon in dream land.

Chapter 23

The next morning… she woke up early.

That was enough rest, and she felt herself again.

She jumped out of bed... and made the coffee.

She had 2 hours, to get ready for Ashton.

Excitement grew in her once again. Her thoughts were of the wonderful time they had together. How they work so well and seem to enjoy a lot of the same things.

Her friends seemed impressed with him also.

That was important to her.

They were her only family.

After a lovely shower, she threw on one of her new sweat suits, and some makeup.

A spray of perfume and touched up her hair.

Now she waits.

There was time, to make sure everything was clean and fresh.

A light dusting and she cleared the few dishes in the sink.

There!.......she was ready.

Sofia Above The Clouds

She stood gazing out her balcony door, at the beautiful day.

The rain had stopped, and the sky was clear.

There was a text message, from Ashton. He was almost there.

Great she replied.

Soon he was at the door.

Hey…….. you look awake and full of life again he laughs

Yes…. I`m back to normal lol. What ever that is. LOL

Ashton had a box, of Croissants, and Pastries.

Kind of a tribute to Paris.

Ohhhh they smell awesome! Sofia sighs.

Mmmmmm

They sat at the table, and Sofia poured the coffee.

I think I got your favorites. I hope so anyway.

They all looked soo good… it was hard to choose.

She laughed.

Once they were settled… Ashton brought up the Cruise.

Soo… you are still interested, right? He questioned.

Have you thought about it at all?

Sofia nodded yes. I thought about it a bit last night.

I know it`s hard for you to picture, but I`ve been on a number of Cruises… and I`m an addict!

Every year… they come out with even bigger and more luxurious ships!

It`s like another world.

Ok.… So, when should we go? Sofia asks.

We`ll have to check with head office. With both of us being gone at the same time, they might be short!

They`ll be fine... Ashton assures her.

The two of them, savored their Pastries.

We`ll be getting more information, this week.

We`ll check it out, then decide what we want to do.

Ok… says Sofia.

I talked to Maina last night. We need to plan our group get together.

They`re dying to hear all about Paris.

I thought… How about a BBQ in our courtyard here.

Soon it will be winter... we only have few more weeks to enjoy it outside.

That sound perfect Ashton agreed.

We should make up a fabulous menu.

Ok… I`ll text Maina and have her call the rest.

What about Saturday… We can start around 4.00.

Sounds good to me he replies.

Ok.

She takes her phone and sends a quick text.

Let us know, when you`ve heard back from the rest.

They sat there, enjoying their coffee.

Sofia speaks up.

That was such a fabulous trip. I feel so fortunate, to be a part of such a great Company.

I`m still in shock.… That`s your parents' company.

It`s a bit overwhelming.

Please don't feel that way! We`re just regular people like anyone.

I hope it doesn`t come between us!

Sofia smiled a sad smile.

No…I care about you. I want us to go slow… and really get to know each other.

These feelings are soo knew to me. Sofia admits.

I`ve spent the last few years, concentrating on my career only.

Yes, I understand.

We`ll take it super slow, and see where it takes us

You`re soo wonderful she says. As long as I don`t ruin it that way.

Thank You for understanding.

Ashton gave her a big hug.

Ok……. Let`s have some fun.

Let`s plan a BBQ!

Sofia grabbed a paper and pen.

Soo what should we have for appetizers?

Something cold because we`ll be outside, and it will be hard
to keep warm.

Of course, we`ll have chips, and nuts.

Well. Ashton thinks.

How about my favorite!   SHRIMP COCKTAIL!

We can have plates ice, to set them on.

Perfect! Done.

Main Meal ***

How about…Italian Sausages

   Dainty Chicken skewers,

     And Salad.

Nice… I`ll make up a tray with mixed veggies.

I like to do red, and green peppers, onions, zucchini,

And mushrooms.

I spread them on a tray….. and roast them with a drizzle of
olive oil.

Wow that sounds delicious Ashton confirms.

That should do it I think.

That covers everyone.

We can make some of those Veggie sausages, for those who

Don`t eat meat too.

Good thinking Sofia nods.

I know Ricky doesn`t.

That was easy…. lol

I`ll call my butcher and have him choose the best products

he has. I`ll ask if he would make me up some small pieces of

Chicken. He carries the biggest shrimp, I`ve ever seen.

I think that covers it.

We can prepare most of it on Friday.

Soo now we have that under control……

How would you like to have dinner tonight, and maybe a

show.

Ohh that sounds good Sofia replies.

I`ll check the cinemas and see what's playing.

There`s a comedy in Cinema 3.

We can just go there and have a bite.

They have Hot Dogs and hamburgers, nachos and tons of

food.

Let's let our hair down….let's just have fun!

And get messy. LOL

They decided on a drive around town, before heading to the show.

Then... Paul dropped them off.

Thanks Paul. I`ll text you when we`re ready.

Have fun kids! He says and drives off.

They went inside… and picked out all kinds of junk food.

The laughed and joked while eating. They even played a few of the kid's games that were there.

Then… they laughed through the movie.

What a fun evening.

They decided, to call it a night so, Ashton asked Paul to head to Sofia`s.

Thanks… she said as they pulled up to her apartment.

That was a blast.

It was wasn`t it!

Maybe we`ll do it again some time.

I hope so Sofia smiles.

She leaned over and gave him a kiss.

Talk to you soon?

For sure Ashton replied.

Good night. … Good night.

Chapter 24

The next day. she got up early and went out to pick up some of the supplies for the BBQ.

All her veggies… chips nuts etc.

Everyone can make it… and it was coming up fast.

She really wanted everything to be perfect.

When she returned home, she went over her list... and check things off.

She made herself a coffee.

She sat at the table in quiet contemplation.

Soo much has happened to her these past few months.

A higher position, in her career,

Traveling to beautiful destinations,

And now a new relationship.

A sudden wave of panic washed over her.

It all started to overwhelm her.

Never in her life, has she had anything she could hold on to.

From the time her parents died, she was placed in foster

care.

The moment she started to feel apart of the family… she would be moved to another.

There was never the sense of belonging.

Tears began flowing from her eyes.

Sofia shook her head. trying to change her train of thought.

Why is she suddenly feeling this way!

She`s been soo happy!

She went into her room, and laid down, staring at the ceiling.

The events in her life, playing out so clearly in her mind.

She started thinking about her feelings for Ashton.

If they get too close, … will she lose him as well?

Suddenly… in the middle of all this good fortune, she `s

Come upon… she`s feeling very confused, and unsure.

The cruise came to her… that would be just a vacation… not part of the job.

That might be a whole different thing.

What will that bring?

Soo many unknown feelings.

How does she handle what may come about?

Light tears still flowing, she reached for a tissue.

She then closed her eyes and drifted off to sleep.

That was a way of escaping her thoughts.

A little while later… she was woken to the sound of her phone ringing.

Hi Sofia… Ashtons voice sounded cheery.

Hi Ashton, she responds.

Ohh you sound a little off... he exclaims.

Are you O K?...

Yaa she replies… just a bit of a head ache. She lied.

It wasn`t like her to lie. She felt bad.

Oh sorry… I just thought maybe we could go for dinner.

But……How about I let you go… and you just get some rest.

Sorry Ashton... Give me a call tomorrow. I should be fine then.

Sure no problem…hope you feel better soon.

Thanks, she replies.

They hung up.

Ashton sits, with a worried look.

Sofia Above The Clouds

He wasn`t sure what to make of that somber conversation.

As soon as she hung up… she called Maina.

She needed her best friend.

She asked her to come over, and Maina agreed.

She had to talk to someone, and break out of this sudden

Attack of nerves.

Maina arrived in no time.

As Sofia opened the door….Maina stepped in and gave her

a hug.

Hey…. What wrong Hun?

What`s going on?

Sofia explained how and why she was feeling that way.

Maina felt soo bad for her.

Sofia fought off more tears.

Maina saw the sadness in her eye…

She felt the confusion.

The best way to help her best friend …is to be truthful.

O K Sofia. I heard every word you said.

Now ...this is my thoughts and feelings about what you`re going through.

For one... What's causing you to feel insecure, is centered around the past.

You were young then and had no say or control.

Secondly...You have grown up and made a very nice life for yourself.

You have a fabulous career, a nice apartment, and you are the one, that made it happen.

Three...This is a completely different situation, from what happened then.

No one can take this away from you now.

You`ve created a whole new life for yourself.

Only you can change that.

Sofia raised her head.

Yaa... I guess you`re right.

You are still just starting out. There will be all kinds of new adventures for you.

You can`t allow the past, to control your future.

Sofia listened intently.

Her tears subsided.

Yes… she said, her eyes growing wider.

You`re right.

The past is gone.

It`s o k Hun… everyone has their moments of un sureness.

I do too. But I just say to hell with it lol.

Remember… you have some great friends. We are always here for you.

You`ll never be alone.

And…… there`s a handsome man, who seems to really have it bad for you.

You are soo lucky! LOL

Sofia light up.

You`re right. I`m being stupid.

Sorry

Don`t be. There are no recipes for life.

We just have to follow our hearts, and instincts.

Not everything will work out …Not everything will turn out as we hope.

We just except it and carry on.

Sofia looked at Maina and says………

I think you should have been a psychiatrist

I feel soo much better now. Everything you said. made sense and is true.

I`m soo glad I called you.

I need this.

Sofia jumped up and poured them another coffee.

I do have a lot of thinking to do.

Soo Maina asks.

How`s the BBQ plans coming along.?

Do you need any help?

No… Ashton and I have our game plan on lol.

The two of them laugh.

Hey…... How about we go over to the mall and have some fun!

SHOPPING ! Sofia shrieks.

Yessssss…… I`m in!

I`ll give Ashton a call when I get home.

I`ll apologize for lying.

Ok… come on. The stores are waiting. LOL

Sofia grabbed her purse... and they took off.
She felt soo much better.

They hailed a Taxi… and too the mall they went!

They spent about two hours in the stores… then stopped for a light meal. They were both famished.
Both came out with a few items. And sat chatting for about an hour.

It was getting late now... 7.00 PM.
Maina had to go.
They quickly called another Taxi and headed back.

Sofia thanked Maina up and down, again, for being there for her.

Then Maina was off.

Once back in her apartment…her thoughts turned to Ashton.

She felt bad.

She`ll give him a call.

Sofia got comfy… and thought of what to say to him.

Then… decided it was best to talk in person.

She picked up her phone and called.

Ashton answered with his usual calm voice.

Hey… are you feeling better?

Yes... Sofia replies. I`m sorry I wasn`t in a mood to talk earlier

How about breakfast in the morning here…we can talk then.

Hesitantly. Ashton asks if there was something wrong.

Oh no... but I`ll explain more tomorrow.

Have I done something? He continues…he was concerned.

No… everything is good.

Ok…Same time?... Would you like those pastries?

Oh Yaa… for sure. I was hoping for you`d bring some LOL

O K I`ll see you then. They hung up.

Sofia got ready for bed… she wanted to be up early.

She was feeling like herself again, and even feeling those butterflies.

Chapter 25

The morning came, and with that, she was excited to have Ashton come over.

She started rehearsing in her head, what she wanted to say to him.

Her mood was positive.

It was getting close.

She dressed in her new jeans, and sweater, from Paris.

They fit nicely.

Then. Hair, and makeup.

There… all set.

She received a text… Ashton was on his way up.

Someone had let him in.

Her excitement grew.

She went to the door. and greeted him.

Good morning…he says.

Good morning! Come in.

Sofia Above The Clouds

Sofia poured the coffee, and Ashton put the goodies on a plate.

Mmm smells like I`ll be gaining weight...LOL

No calories Ashton joked!

It`s good to see you laugh today...I was a bit worried yesterday, Ashton admits.

Sofia smiled. Yaa... I want to explain.

She told Ashton what happened and apologized for lying.

I was just on a spot.

She went on to tell him what happened.

I asked you before... if we could take it slow.

Now...I really feel like that even more.

All my life...anytime I felt I was a part of anyone's life...

They were taken away.

I was moved from one foster home to another.

There was never a feeling of belonging, or security.

Anyone I ever started to feel close to, just went away.

Tears, slowly welled up in Sofia`s eyes.

Sorry she said, as she wiped them away.

Soo when I realized how much I enjoyed being with you…

and how I`ve been growing closer and closer…

It brought back all those feelings.

Then… I began to fear you leaving as well.

I don`t know…. If was just crazy. That never happened to

me before.

Maybe because all I`ve thought about was my career for the

last few years.

Suddenly … you came out of nowhere lol.

A relationship was the last thing on my mind.

Now… I have all these feelings!

It must have been buried inside.

 Soo I`m sorry.

For what! Ashton stood up and puts his arms around her.

Don`t ever apologize! It`s not your fault!

I know… but I wanted you to know, how I feel.

Soo. Sofia speaks very slow…...

If you`d rather not go on any further… I`ll understand.

Sofia Above The Clouds

Ashton held her closer.

Are you serious? I feel closer to you now, then ever!

I`m not going anywhere…he pauses….

Not unless you want me to leave. His face turned serious.

Sofia shook her head. Noooooooooo

O k whew……

Soo.. How about we change this subject….not to make light
of it…

And go over our list for the BBQ in two days!

Sofia nodded with a huge smile.

Yes…...I`m done with tears.

Thank You for understanding… Sofia sighs.

They hugged and got to work.

I`ve been eyeing the weather… so far soo good.

Oh yaa I hope so.

They crossed everything they had off the list.

I`ll be picking up the order from the deli, in the morning.

I`ll come right here after that… to put together.

Great says Sofia.

I`ll sauté some onions too.

Good Idea. Ashton remarks I love them!

I want to put the Chicken and veggie skewers together.

Then set up the shrimp cocktails.

I thought a nice char cautery Board would be nice.

Oh wow…… now that`s what I love! LOL

This party is going to be a big hit!

Ok Sofia… I`m going to take off…. I have some errands to run.

I will be here in the morning. And we`ll get everything prepared!

Sounds good. Should be fun, watching you in the kitchen lol

Yaa well you wait!. I`m not that bad, you know?

I make a mean steak too!

Sofia laughs…. o k

She walked him to the door.

Ashton gave her a hug and kiss.

Everything will be just great…. This is your new beginning.

I`m with you all the way… soo

Sofia smiled

You`re the best. Thank You

I`ll be here for 10.00 Am... Ashton calls back as he heads down the hall.

Perfect she calls back.

Talk Later.

Sofia closed the door…and ran to her phone.

She had to call Maina!

Maina answers out of breath!

Ohh hi Hun… I just got in the door.

How are you doing? She asked.

Sofia informed her of what she did… and told her she felt better than ever!

All thanks to you.

Noo you just needed someone to assure you.

You`ll be O K.

Yaa I needed to get that sorted out… in order to make a new start.

Soo I just had to fill you in.

I`m soo looking forward to Saturday…. we have a fabulous menu!

You`ll love it!

Well, I`ll come a bit early, to give you a hand.

Ohh that would be great…. O K… I`ll see you then.

Tomorrow…. Ashton and I are getting thing prepared.

 OK Can`t wait….

They hung up.

Sofia decided to do some cleaning, then changed the sheets on her bed.

She`d better do some laundry too.

She was filled with energy!

She thought of Saturday… while she flew around her apartment.

She thought too, of the Cruise.

This time…her feelings were positive.

She felt a new sense of emotions.

This was different!

It`s now almost dinner time. She was getting hungry

She`ll have a busy two days coming up… so She took her phone… and Chinese it was.

Beef and green peppers… honey garlic spareribs…and 2 egg rolls.

Mmm!

She freshened up and got comfortable while she awaited her delivery.

Once it arrived, she pretty much inhaled half of it... the rest she savored while watching a light comedy.

Soon after... her eyes began to close.

It was time.

She headed for her bed.... And that was that.

Sofia went into a deep peaceful sleep.

A well-deserved sleep.

No dreams tonight.

Chapter 26

Just as the night…the morning came what seemed like instantly.

She jumped up and got into the shower.

After going through her usual morning ritual… she began bringing everything out for preparation, when Ashton arrives.

She added 2 extensions into her table, so there was lots of room.

She then. Sorted through her fridge…so they could easily set things out... with easy access.

She soon got her text….

Ashton was on his way.

She ran to the bathroom, and double checked her hair and makeup.

She gave herself a little spray of a light scented perfume. `

The doorbell rang, and she let him in.

Hey…...Good Morning! here… let me help you.

Ashton was carrying a big box, and a number of bags.

They set them on the counter.

Let`s have a coffee first.

Sounds great Ashton replies…I haven`t had any yet.

Oh Yaa?.......I don`t leave my place with out at least two

lolol

Sofia laughs.

Well, I have it ready so you`re in luck.

Soo my dear…Ashton changes the subject…I say, after we finish what we're doing here….., we look over the Cruise details. They came this morning.

You do still want to go right?

Ashton looks hopeful.

You know what? ...Sofia looks right at him.

I want to go now… more than ever!

Ohh…you had me scared for a minute there!

Awesome he lets out a sigh of relief.

They unwrapped… all their items and started to prepare.

They had fun while they worked.

Sofia watched Ashton, as he meticulously made up his skewers.

They DID look very appetizing she admitted.

He coated them in an array of seasonings.

Thank you, Ashton replies with confidence.

He looked and felt proud.

She left him, to do his thing….and went back to hers.

When everything was prepped and ready…they placed them in the fridge.

Time for a break.

Ashton reached for the envelope from head office.

He was anxious to see the details.

Sofia sat across from him and waited.

O K…. It says, The next Cruise out… is Monday!

Seven days.

It's the largest in the world.

There will be 4 Islands that we visit.

If we choose… there are arrangements in place, so that we can stay on an additional seven days… travelling in the opposite direction, and different Islands.

We`ll have five days to decide.

Wow. Sofia's eyes widened. I had forgotten you mentioned that.

I`ll do whatever you feel like.

I`ve never been… and you have many times.
I`ll just follow whatever you decide.

O K then Ashton sets the papers down.
I`ll let them know…to make our flight arrangements as well.

Ohh Awesome. We`re really going!

We`ll be flying into Port Canaveral.
They`ll have transportation to and from.
When they finalize everything… Kyle will send our Itinerary.
I`m getting excited now.
That's only three days away…. OMG!

I`d better go through my summer wardrobe quickly.
Wow!

First things First!
Tomorrow, we have our BBQ
It will be fun!

Soo… Sofia suddenly thinks of something!

Will they be left short? With both of us gone.

Noo Ashton states.

They will bring in a couple from the main airline.

There is a list of volunteers… who have been filling if. For years.

All well experienced.

Soo we`re good.

I think I mentioned earlier. So, you wouldn`t worry…. but I didn`t elaborate.

They have quite a set up in place.

Yes… it sounds they do! LOL

Our company cares as much about their staff… as they do the Guests.

That`s why … when we took on an unexpected trip, to cover for Kaylee…they rewarded us with the Cruise.

We were scheduled for our down time then.

But… we didn`t hesitate.

My Father does not believe in overworking his employees.

That`s never a good thing.

He put a number of scenarios together and came up with the right solutions.

I must admit!... He`s a smart man.

Yes… it sounds like he knows what he`s doing alright.

I feel even more proud to be a part of this company.

I still don`t know how I managed to be here… but I`m soo glad …. And grateful.

Ashton smiled. That big, sweet smile… and Sofia smiled in return.

It`s funny, you know… when I think back…

I had heard talk of this company. from other Hostesses.

I didn`t quite know what it was really about.

I was soo busy just trying to do my best and keep my job.

I only had myself for support.

I couldn`t risk getting too involved with gossip, or cheap talk.

Well…. Ashton remarks!

It looks like it paid off for you. You succeeded!

Soo who`s the smart one?

I just do my best Ashton.

I will always be loyal to where I work.

I`ll always give 100%!

I know that…Ashton agrees.

I watch you with the guests…. No matter who they are,

You treat them with respect.

Anytime we`ve worked together… you`ve always done your job, and then some.

Sofia looked puzzled.

I never noticed that…. Hmm.

She laughs. I guess I do get fully into my work lol.

O k…. so now.. what`s next. Have we got everything we need?

Yaa It looks like it to me, Ashton replies.

How about I order us a pizza…...and after that… I will leave you to your day.

I`m just starving! .LOL

Oh, that sound good to me. I haven`t had pizza in forever!

O k……How about Paesano's.

I've had theirs before… and it was pretty good.

Sure…Just order whatever you like.

I love it all Sofia shrugs.

I`ll have anything on my pizza.

Dons. It will be here in 30 minutes.

Can I help you with anything else? Ashton offered.

No.. I think I'm good thanks.

Let's take a coffee on the balcony.

 It looks nice out.

Awww…. This is good.

I think we`re getting down to our last few weeks of nice weather.

Maybe less.

That`s O K… All I care about is that tomorrow is good for the BBQ. LOL

Sofia laughs. I`m really looking forward to this.

The only one I`ve seen.. is Maina.

We took off to fast… to see anyone else.

Just no time.

Yaa… That`s right! Ashton nods.

They will be needing their Sofia fix! LOL

Ha Ha Ha… You`re so funny Sofia grins.

Although … you`re also probably right! They

Both laughs.

Oh look... here comes our pizza! Great... I`m so hungry.

Ashton just went down to the front and met him there.

Saved him a trip up the elevator.

Sofia put out a couple of plates.

Wow ... smell so good!

Would you like a pop… or anything to drink? She asks.

No.. I`m still nursing my coffee.

I just want PIZZA! LOL

OMG... Sofia laughs! You are hungry! Lol

They both devoured that poor pizza.

Ahhhhh… That was to dye for! Ashton sings out.

Just like before. Great choice she agreed.

It was awesome.

You`ll have to leave me that number.

One night when Maina is over… we`ll have this for a

change.

She`ll love it I`m sure!

Ashton cut out the part of the box, that had the name and number.

She could just keep it in her junk drawer in the kitchen.

O K…. I think this is my cue… to head out.

I want to start packing for the Cruise as well.

Tomorrow we`ll be tied up.

That only leaves Sunday.

Sooo…I`ll be here early to help out Ashton says.

Try and get to sleep early… You`ll be soo busy

Before everyone comes.

Yaa I will she responds. I want to enjoy the day.

Ok…. I`ll see you around 2.00

That will give us lots of time.

Ashton gave her a kiss.

Thanks a lot … Sofia tells him. It`s kind of nice not having to do everything myself.

This is fun. We work well together, just like at work…lol

O K. See you then. She shuts the door.

There was a smile on her face. She ran to the balcony… and watched as he disappeared.

That was weird?... she thought to herself!

Why did I just do that LOL.

She shook her head.

She gave Maina a call... and talked while puttering around in her closet.

She was pulling out her warm weather clothes again.

They chit chatted for about an hour…then hung up.

She lined up what she found… and folded them up and into her open suitcase.

She also packed a couple sweaters and a jacket.

Then… she took out her travel necessities. And made sure they were filled up.

Her favorite shampoo, and conditioner, some bath oil, etc.

She opened a new tooth paste and brush.

Then... she packed her sandals, running shoes, slippers, and 2 nice sun hats.

She stopped there, not knowing what else she might need.

Maybe Ashton can help her there.

Ok……I`m done for today.

There`s not much left to pack I don`t think

Sofia Above The Clouds

Maybe I`ll go for a walk.

I could use the exercise… and to burn off that pizza! Lol

It could be the last time, before the real cold sets in.

She left… and must have walked for over an hour.

That was enough fresh air she thought lol.

The rest of the day…was just relaxing.

She laid on the couch…and put a nice movie on.

Her fingers were crossed, for nice weather tomorrow.

The night, soon turned into morning.

Chapter 27

She woke up on the couch.… but that was o k.

She had a real good sleep.

Quite a long one too. It was probably all the fresh air from her walk.

She headed into the shower, and got dressed.

Once the coffee was mad…. she sat and enjoyed thinking about the hours to come.

Her get togethers, were always soo important to her.

Her friends gave her that family feel she soo longed for.

Today… she and Ashton will tell them all about Paris…and then…the Cruise.

Deep down… she still wonders what she ever did, to get this lucky!

She went to her phone… and called Yvonne.

She verified with her about taking care of things while they were Cruising.

Yvonne said no problem… and Sofia mentioned that she wasn`t sure yet if it would be 1 or 2 weeks.

That didn`t make any difference to Yvonne.

Oh great … Thank You soo much.

Sofia had a little gift for her too, which she will leave by one of the plants.

She`ll find it there for sure.

Sofia checked the weather forecast…it still looked good.

There was a slight chance of rain… but not till later on in the evening.

She headed down to the courtyard…to see if they would have to do any cleaning up. But it was all clear.

While she was there. She ran into Lenora.

Lenora was watering the flowers.

Hello!... Sofia approached her. Are you all settled in?

Lenora turned and with a nice smile said…. Oh yes.

It doesn`t take me very long.

I`ve learned to downsize… and eliminate whenever I move.

Hopefully this is my last LOL

You must find that tiering!

Yaa it can be. You lose friends and have to start all over finding your way around, and your favorite foods in a new grocery store. LOL

New York is not very good... for getting to places quick.

But…I just except that and carry on.

Sofia mentioned that she`d be gone, for the next couple of weeks, possibly.

They would for sure meet up then.

Oh... Have you met Yvonne yet?

She`s such a nice neighbor. You two would make great friends.

She`s also alone. I`m sure she would love someone close to get together with.

Lenora mentioned that they had briefly met in the hall, but hadn`t really had a chance.

Well…...Sofia adds.

When I get back… I`ll have you both over.

And… if you happen to meet up sooner… that would even be great.

Oh… that`s so nice of you. I can tell already… I have one perfect neighbor.

Sofia just smiled. No… I just hate seeing people alone.

I know that feeling all too well.

Ok... It was nice running into you again!

If there`s anything you need… just let me know.

Oh thank you… and you have a great trip.

A cruise did you say? They are the best vacation you could have.

You get the best of everything.

The sound of the waves, never leave me.

I`ve been on many times.

My husband loved to cruise. Abut when he died… I never had it in me to go back.

Besides… I didn`t have anyone to go with.

Ohhh that`s too bad.

I heard they have singles cruises. Maybe you could try one.

Yaa... I thought about it one year, but never went.

Well.. you never know what comes up in life. Maybe you`ll meet someone who also loves them.

Sofia smile, with a look of hope.

Well... I`d better get back.

We`ll catch up when I`m home.

Yes, says Lenora! Looking forward to it.

Just have fun and enjoy every minute of your Cruise.

You said it was your first…...You`re going to be in awe.

Wait till you step on board.

I can`t wait.

Talk soon.

Sofia headed back to her apartment.

 She sat back down at the table… and began texting her friends.

She wanted to make sure, they were all coming, and that there were no problems.

Everyone is a go.

Surprisingly. even Angel was able to make it.

Her hectic schedule at the hospital made it difficult

A lot of the time.

As a nurse and surgical nurse…she was always in demand.

Sofia had met her, years ago…. when she had twisted an ankle.

Angel was on duty in the E.R.

They just seemed so connect… and from there became

friends.

There was a bit of time left before Ashton will arrive…

She decided to have a little rest… to rejuvenate.

She grabbed her pillow off the bed… and a small blanket.

She just wanted an hour or so.

With everything ready… and a clear mind.…

Sofia fell into a wonderful sleep.

She was awoken, about an hour and a half later... to her phone ringing.

It was Ashton. Hey sweety… how`s it going there he sounds cheery.

Ohh hi.… It`s great. When are you coming?

Soon.. I thought I`d stop and pick up some ice.

Oh yaa … good thinking thank you.

That should be it.

Ok... I`ll be there in about half an hour.

Perfect Sofia replies. See you then.

Sofia freshened up, and changed into her more dressy Jeans… and black sweater.

Her blonde hair really gave her that sexy look… but, not too sexy.

She applied some soft makeup, and her new Channel perfume.

She was ready for the BBQ

Chapter 28

Ashton soon was at her door.

She greeted him with a big hug. He then put the ice in the freezer.

Soo...What is there left to do ...he asks?

Just bring everything to the courtyard and fire up the BBQ.

We can have things started... and set up for drinks.

That's easy.

Are you staring to pack for our Cruise yet?

Ashton laughs. This is beginning to be a habit LOL.

Last minute trips.

At least this one is just for fun... and relaxation.

No waiting on guests... in fact we're the guests being served! That's a nice treat.

Oh, Yaa Sofia agrees. I think we need that.

I'm starting to get excited he says.

It's been a little while.

I spoke to my new neighbor, in the courtyard a while ago.

She said she loves to Cruise also.

She hasn't been in a few years since her husband died

though.

I found that soo sad.

I`ll be talking to her more when we get back.

Since she and Yvonne are both alone… they should get to know each other.

Maybe they could travel together! Who knows.

Anyway, she seems very nice.

Sofia and Ashton began bringing everything down to the courtyard.

Ashton also brought a folding table... to put his food and accessories on.

There were a few picnic tables already there for use, by anyone who lives there.

It was nice that the flowers were still in color also.

That made it a really nice background.

Any later… and they would be finished.

Sofia figured that by the time they get back… the scenery would be gone.

They set out the drink glasses... and filled some bowls with everyone's favorites.

Chips. And dip…nuts…...her favorite...Fritos1 …

She would have to have restraint over herself. LOL

Sofia remained with the food... while Ashton made a couple trips back and forth. He brought down, the long trough like dish…what ever it is called, to fill with ice for the shrimp.

He set them out very meticulously so that they looked like they were from a 5-star restaurant.

They were huge!

Next.. he placed his chicken skewers in an ice tray as well.

The sausages were bathing in BBQ sauce, that he made himself.

They smelled awesome.

They had a variety of wines, and plates of cheese.

The charcuterie Board was placed on top of another plate of ice… until everyone arrived.

Everything was pretty much set up, when her friends started to arrive.

They greeted each other with hugs and kisses.

Maina was first.

Sorry I couldn`t come earlier she said. I was on a long-distance call.

My cousin just wouldn`t shut up! Lol

That`s ok… we did just fine together. Sofia nodded.

All is good! Have a glass of wine.

Sure…. I`m ready for that!

They laughed.

Fredric and Ricardo…showed up next. Flowers and kisses
Were given.

Oh… guys… you didn`t have to do that! They`re soo
beautiful.

They never come empty handed. Both are such gentlemen
and show great educate.

Ashton walked towards them... and shook their hands.

Nice to see you again!

Wine? they nodded and picked up their glasses.

What service!... they laughed.

Thank You. Kind sir!

Mmm…Ricky says. Smells so good! Wow!

That`s my BBQ sauce Ashton smiles.

Don`t even ask how I make it. It`s family secret.

He laughs.

Well, it`s smells very good! Fred commented.

Just then… Kaylee and Angel appeared.

Het guys…

Sofia ran over and hugged them both. I`m soo glad

You were able to come Angel!

I never know for sure. If you get called into work for an

emergency.

I made sure... I covered my ass today! LOL

Well that`s great!... you need a break anyway.

Ladies…get your glasses. I'm pouring! LOL

Peter arrived a moment later.

Hey…   Glad you made it Hun!

Sofia hugged him and motioned for him to get a glass.

The tray of BBQ sausages were just fantastic!

Ashton had them on low.

The aroma filled the air.

Wow guys… you went all out here… Peter comments.

Everything looks wonderful!

Thanks Sofia answers.

I hope you enjoy!

She then, uncovers the Charcuterie Board.

It looked amazing! It was just covered in all the best items.

Dipping sauces on the side.

French bread sliced perfectly.

A work of art!

OMG… did you make this yourself? Ricky`s eyes were wide.

I did! Sofia responded.

Have you ever given a thought to a catering business? LOL

Actually… just before, I went in for Airline Hostess…I did have thoughts of that.

I didn`t have the finances to pursue it though.

I find… it brings out the creativity in me.

It`s very satisfying.

Well, it looks fabulous1

Ashton poured Himself and Sofia a wine.

CHEERS guys!

We have lots of good food here, and it will be ready soon.

CHEERS they all rang out.

They had moved the tables together, so it was easier to talk.

Ricky and Fred like the way it was set up.

This is perfect. Just the right number of seats... with room to move!

Sofia proceeded to bring out the Shrimp.

Wow... those are huge! Maina shrieked.

Everyone`s eye opened wide!

Where the hell did you find those my dear...Fred had a look of amazement.

Ashton has a Deli Shop he loves. The owner seems to love him LOL He only serves him the best of the best.

That`s because, we`ve been dealing with him for years and years.

He`s like part of the family! Ashton laughs.

We send him tons of business.

Ok... I think everything is ready!

Ashton puts out the trays of Sausage, chicken skewers, and

the tray Sofia made up with the roasted veggies.

He opened the fresh bakery rolls…. And butter.

Everyone takes a plate…. And dig in!
There`s lots.

While they headed for the serving table…Sofia went around and topped up the drinks.
For a moment there ..she felt like she was at work LOL
But no…. not even close.

As they sat with their plates loaded up with goodies…
They requested Sofia fills them in on her unexpected trip to Paris.

So… she did. She gave a descript run down on everything.
The hotel… the shopping…. the ambiance …
She described the Food… the Eiffel Tower, The Louvre.

Then the Spa… that transported then to another world!
Her friends sat in intense silence.
Wow what a trip! Ricky speaks up.
Sounds amazing!

Yes… we had the best time yet!

She sat with a smile, ear to ear! A low giggle was hard to

Hide.

Wait! ..Maina demanded!

There`s something more! Isn`t there?

What haven`t you told us?

Everyone gazed at Sofia.

Well…. there was something that happened, that even I

have trouble believing!

What!!!! Tell us.

Ok…. So. On the plane, I had a very distinguished

gentleman, speak to me.

He said that he though I was beautiful… and if I was

interested in fashion! Of course, I said yes!

Well… he mentioned that a very good friend of his, was a

designer in Paris! Then asked if I might be interested in

backstage tickets… if he had a shop going on.

OMG…. Don`t tell us you went to a runway show in

Paris!!!!!!!

Sofia paused, leaving them hanging!   LOL

Come on… did you? Maina seemed anxious.

Sort of. Sofia laughs.

It was better that that!!! Everyone was frozen waiting.

I was actually in the show! Everyone`s mouths dropped open.

WHAT!!!!!!!!

 Yes….. I ended up modeling the Show Stopper.!

Ashton took over the conversation.

He mentioned what had happened, and how Sofia came to be a model.

OMG… What an experience!!!

Ohh Yaa…It was surreal!

At the end…. Sofia was given the Wedding Gown, she had modeled!

What an experience that must have been… Fred blurted out.

I can`t believe you never told me Maina screams!

Sofia Above The Clouds

How did you keep that to yourself! LOL
I would have screamed it out the second I got home!
Wow!

I`m still in disbelief myself!... Sofia shook her head.

Kaylee pouted. Yaa that was supposed to be MY trip!
Of course, I had to be sick!
Yaa I`m sorry Kaylee.

Don`t be… I`m glad it was you who covered for me.
No one better.

Thanks Hun!. . Maybe you`ll get another trip like that soon.
Yaa who knows she shrugged.

Ashton winked at Sofia. Sofia smiled.

Yaa… I`m sure, something will come along just as nice.

Neither Kaylee, nor anyone else knows who Ashton really
is.

No one else put it together.

It was better that way, for the time being anyway.

It felt exciting to Sofia… to have a secret just between the two of them.

It felt like a special bond.

The evening played out with fun and laughter!

Their dinner was a huge success!

The Cruise was brought up, and they informed the group about leaving on Monday!

They said it would be 1 or 2 weeks.

Yaa O K… Soo two weeks you`ll be gone. LOL

Probably Ashton smiled at Sofia.

That`s what I'm hoping, but Sofia has the final word LOL

Everyone laughed.

So should I book our favorite area at Alexanders for then? Ricky laughs.

Oh yes… for sure Ashton stated. We`ll count on that.

Ashton fit in with them so well.

At one point… Fred went and sat beside him, and told him, how he felt about Sofia.

She like our little sister, he says.

We feel she`s in good hands with you.

Please be good to her. She needs someone like you.

She`s had a rough enough time in the past.

Yes… Ashton nods. She told me all about that.

Can I tell you a secret Ashton leans closer to Fred.

Don`t say anything to anyone, but…..I`m in total love with her. We had a long conversation, and she said she wanted to take things slow.

I agree.

But……. When the time comes, I will ask her to marry me.

Fred turned towards him.

I wish you the best. From the way she looks at you… and talks about you…I think it will happen.

Just take your time… and let her really get to know you.

Ashton nodded... I will he said. I have nothing but respect for her… so as long as it takes….

I think we are all going to be very close friends! Ashton says.

Yaa I think we will.

Thanks for the talk!...

Ashton got up to offer more refills.

Fred felt like he made a new friend…. He did.

He was happy for Sofia.

It was approaching midnight by this time.

They decided it was time to call it a night.

They all pitched in, to clean up, and bring everything back up to the apartment.

Sofia appreciated that.

She was getting tired.

It went very easy, and quick.

Then they said they`re good nights.

They wished Sofia and Ashton a great trip!

Thanks guys… .Ohhh wait….

Sofia ran to her bedroom and brought out the bag of trinkets for them all.

I almost forgot.

Sofia Above The Clouds

I was planning on having them at the dinner LOL
Too much to remember.

They thanked her and made their exit.
Ashton stayed and helped Sofia put everything away.
The leftovers went into the fridge… with some… in the freezer.
They took all the garbage, down to the garbage room in the building.

When everything was away… Ashton said good night.
Sofia thanked him again for all huis help, and the fabulous food.
I think you were a major hit… she announced.
Well I hope so…because I just adore your friends.

You have a great sleep… and I`ll call you in the afternoon.

With that…. He turned and left.

Sofia got ready… and with a sigh of contentment.
Fell off to sleep

Chapter 29

The next morning… as she sat on her balcony, enjoying her coffee, Sofia had soo many thoughts circling her mind.

The past couple months have been a whirlwind of changes.

Her new career… new relationship….

Confessing her inner struggles…. The list goes on.

She went over her trips… with both Kaylee, and Ashton.

The past was also rearing its head again.

Now… the CRUISE!

Another brand-new experience.

This time… it isn`t work!

She played out different scenarios in her mind.

She was suddenly afraid, of what she had asked of Ashton.

Taking it very slow. What if they get caught up in a moment…and he gets frustrated with her.

What if he gets board of just being close friends?

And…. What if he just decides to give up on her… and leave like everyone else did in the past!

This Cruise could mean do or die for them.

This Cruise will let her know… how strong their newfound bond really is.

Tomorrow will be the start of a whole new chapter for her.

Will they stand the test of time?

 Will love win, or the harsh reality of being apart catch up with them?

Will they grow even close?

What new adventures await them on board one of the largest ships in the world!

That will be an entirely different experience.

She`ll be on the Seas… not in the clouds!

She`ll find out soon enough if what awaits her is an adventure or something else!

The waves were bringing in something for her, and every flow had a message coming towards her at full speed and charge.

Watch out for the second book to come.

The story unfolds the hidden secret that is yet to be told.

No one Knows!